PREACHER
salvation ™

GARTH ENNIS
writer

STEVE DILLON
artist

PAMELA RAMBO
colorist

CLEM ROBINS
letterer

original covers by
GLENN FABRY

featuring pinups by

PREACHER created by GARTH ENNIS and STEVE DILLON

SALVATION,TX
POP. 1626

GLENN FAB

SIX MONTHS LATER

THERE COMES A TIME, SKEETER OL' BOY...

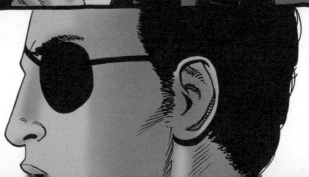

WHEN YOU JUST PLAIN RUN OUT OF AMERICA.

THE MAN FROM GOD KNOWS WHERE

GARTH ENNIS-Writer STEVE DILLON-Artist

Pamela Rambo-Colorist, Clem Robins-Letterer, Axel Alonso-Editor

PREACHER created by Garth Ennis and Steve Dillon

SIX
MONTHS
EARLIER:

SALVATION TX.
POPN. 1626

JODIE'S BAR & G

COMIN'?

WUFF!

LONE STAR 'N A SHOT.

SURE, DUDE.

SHOULDN'T THAT BE A PARROT?

MM?

I ALWAYS HEARD PIRATES HAD PARROTS, Y'KNOW? LIKE, PIECES OF EIGHT! PIECES OF EIGHT!

I MEAN HELL, YOU DONE THE EYE AN' ALL, WHY NOT GO ALL THE WAY?

AW, HE'S STILL A LITTLE DRUNK FROM LAST NIGHT--

OR A HOOK! HOW ABOUT A HOOK?

YA-HARR, JIM-LAD!

C'MON, DAVY, LEAVE HIM BE...

DUDE, THE GUY'S TRYNNA--

DAMN THIS HOOK, JIM-LAD! WENT TO SCRATCH ME EYE AN' NOW LOOK AT ME, YA-HARR! AN' WHEN I WENT TO TAKE A LEAK--

SHOULDN'T YOU HAVE A HAND UP YOUR ASS?

HUH?

I ALWAYS HEARD MISS PIGGY HAD A HAND UP HER ASS.

DAVY--!

OH, CAP'N BLACKBEARD'S A COMEDIAN...

WALK AWAY, BOY.

WHO THE FUCK ARE YOU CALLIN'--

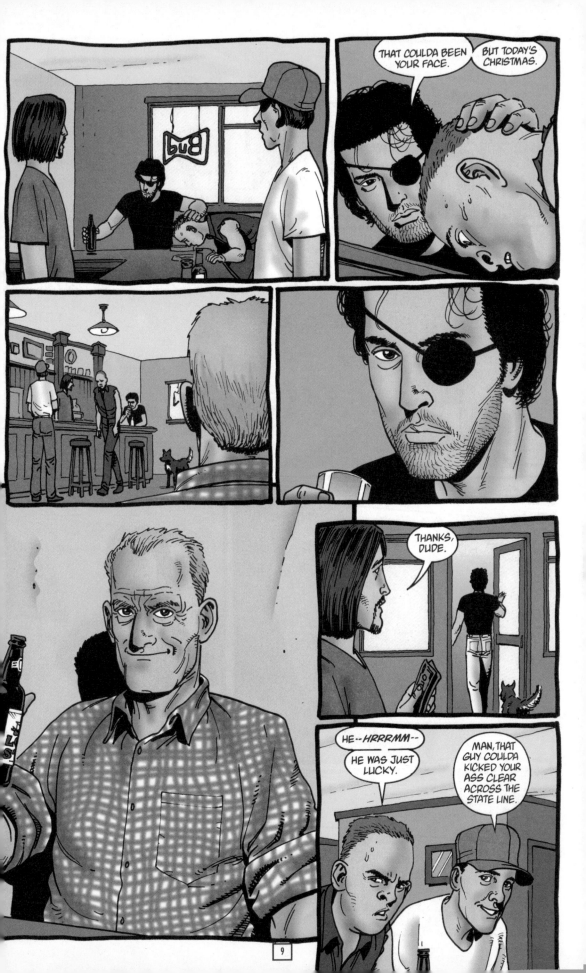

HEY! CYCLOPS!!

C'MON, HONEY, GIVE US A LOOK AT IT!

WHAT THE FUCK ARE YOU, FROM STAR TREK OR SOMETHIN'?

THEY LET YOU OUT FOR THE DAY, EYEBALL? HAW!

FUCKIN' MUTATED BITCH--

PLEASE! STOP IT! STOP IT!

WHY CAN'T YOU JUST LEAVE ME ALONE?!

LORIE--?

WHAT THE FUCK DO YOU WANT?

SORRY, MISS--

SORRY--

WON'T DO IT AGAIN, EVER--

SWEAR TO GOD--

YOU OKAY, LORIE? MISS BOBBS?

I AM NOW, THANK YOU...UM...

PARDON ME, BUT DO I KNOW YOU?

LONG TIME AGO YOU DID. JESSE CUSTER.

YOUR BROTHER BILLY-BOB'S FRIEND? WHEN WE WERE KIDS?

UM...

JESSE...?

BUT--BUT YOU LOOK SO DIFFERENT! I'D NEVER HAVE RECOGNIZED YOU IN A MILLION YEARS!

YEAH, WELL, I HAD A LITTLE ACCIDENT...

NO, I MEAN YOU LOOK COMPLETELY DIFFERENT! YOU'RE LIKE A NEW MAN!

I MEAN YOU WERE TALL EVEN THEN, WELL OVER SIX FEET, AND YOU WERE SO GOOD-LOOKING...

AND YOUR EYES USED TO BE BROWN, DIDN'T THEY? AND YOUR HAIR--WHAT HAPPENED TO ALL THAT BEAUTIFUL SHINY BLACK HAIR YOU HAD?

UH, WELL, LONG AS I'M HERE, LEMME GIVE YOU A RIDE HOME...

OH, BUT I LIVE JUST RIGHT AROUND THE CORNER--

IT'S NO TROUBLE.

WE CAN'T JUST STAND BY AND--

I SAID: LEAVE IT.

BUT HE BEAT THE HELL OUTTA THEM RIGHT IN THE STREET!

DIDN'T HE, THOUGH.

MA'AM.

HMMMM.

NO, MY DADDY WAS MAD ABOUT IT FOR A LONG TIME, PROBABLY STILL IS. BUT I REMEMBERED YOU AND BILLY-BOB FROM WHEN YOU WERE LITTLE KIDS. I KNEW YOU'D NEVER DO ANYTHING TO HURT HIM...

MEANS A LOT TO HEAR YOU SAY THAT, LORIE. EVEN NOW.

HE CAN STAY IN THE TRUCK...

NO, HE'S FINE. HE'S A SWEET LITTLE GUY.

WUFF!

IT WASN'T TOO LONG AFTER THAT I LEFT HOME, ACTUALLY. I WANTED TO GO TO COLLEGE AND STUDY FOR A BUSINESS DEGREE, BUT ...WELL, YOU'VE SEEN HOW PEOPLE CAN BE. THERE WEREN'T TOO MANY PLACES WANTED ME AROUND CAMPUS.

BUT I TAUGHT MYSELF A LOT FROM BOOKS AND THINGS. AND JODIE HELPED ME GET THROUGH THE TESTS --IT'S AMAZING, REALLY. JODIE KNOWS JUST ABOUT EVERYTHING.

JODIE, HUH?

YES, COME IN AND SAY HELLO!

GOD DAMMIT, LORENA ...YOU EVER GOING TO LEARN ANY CONSIDERATION FOR MY FUCKING HANGOVER...?

WHO'S THIS?

JODIE, I'D LIKE YOU TO MEET JESSE CUSTER.

EVENIN', MA'AM.

MY, SUCH MANNERS. A REGULAR HANDSOME STRANGER.

SOME OF THOSE AWFUL QUINCANNON MEN WERE GIVING ME TROUBLE AGAIN, JODIE. JESSE SAVED ME-- HE REALLY TAUGHT THEM A LESSON, HONESTLY!

KNIGHT IN SHINING ARMOR, TOO. WELL, I GUESS THAT DESERVES A DRINK...

I'LL MAKE SOME TEA.

GOT SOME- THING STRONGER THROUGH HERE. THE MUTT YOURS?

YEAH.

HE BETTER NOT SHIT ON THE CARPET.

14

YOU GOT SOME NICE STUFF...

PAINTINGS AND POTS ARE MOSTLY LORIE'S, BOOKS ARE MINE. I READ A LOT.

THANK YOU...YEAH, ME TOO. THAT SOME KINDA LEATHERBOUND COPY'VE CATCH-22 I SEE THERE?

ENGLISH EDITION. GOT SOME GOOD LINE DRAWINGS IN IT.

HOW'D YOU LOSE THE EYE, STRANGER?

TELL YOU THE TRUTH, I DON'T RIGHTLY KNOW.

KINDA CARELESS WITH YOUR BODY PARTS, AIN'T YOU?

MAKES TWO'VE US.

HELL, I KNOW EXACTLY WHAT HAPPENED TO THAT. GODDAMN GATOR BIT IT OFF IN THE SWAMP.

JODIE... HEY, THAT PLACE ON THE MAIN STREET YOURS? BOY BEHIND THE BAR CALLS FELLAS *DUDE* WITHOUT CHECKIN' IF THEY OBJECT OR NOT?

MINE AND LORIE'S. I RUN IT, SHE DOES THE BOOKS. THAT GIRL'S A MATHEMATICAL GENIUS, I TELL YOU.

WHERE DO YOU KNOW HER FROM, ANYWAY?

WE KINDA GREW UP TOGETHER--ME AN' HER BROTHER, ANYHOW.

FUNNY THING WAS, SHE DIDN'T SEEM TO RECOGNIZE ME. NOT ONE BIT.

THAT'S BECAUSE OF HER EYE CONDITION.

SOMEONE OR OTHER'S SYNDROME, I DON'T KNOW THE EXACT DETAILS. BASICALLY, THE EYES --WELL, THE EYE--SOMETIMES IT SENDS THE WRONG INFORMA- TION TO THE BRAIN. YOU LOOK AT ONE THING, BUT YOU SEE SOMETHING ELSE ALTOGETHER.

HERE WE ARE... JESSE, ARE YOU IN A HURRY TO GET SOMEWHERE?

NO...

WELL, WE HAVE A SPARE ROOM UP- STAIRS. WHY DON'T YOU STAY HERE TONIGHT AND THEN MAKE A FRESH START IN THE MORNING?

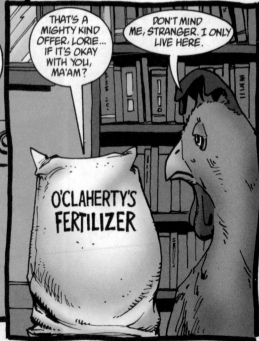

THAT'S A MIGHTY KIND OFFER, LORIE... IF IT'S OKAY WITH YOU, MA'AM?

DON'T MIND ME, STRANGER. I ONLY LIVE HERE.

O'CLAHERTY'S FERTILIZER

AM I IN A HURRY TO GET SOMEWHERE...

AM I SHIT.

AIN'T ABOUT TA GO... QUITTIN' ON ME, ARE YA, PILGRIM?

HELL, NO, I AIN'T ABOUT TO QUIT ON YOU. ANY TIME NOW I'M GONNA CHOKE DOWN THIS BIG OL' SHIT SANDWICH I BEEN SERVED AN' SHOULDER MY GOD-DAMN BURDEN AGAIN, KEEP ON TRYNNA ACCOM-PLISH THE IMPOSSIBLE.

ANY TIME NOW.

AN' WHAT THE HELL IS THAT SUPPOSED TO MEAN?

MEANS I CAN'T KEEP ON DOIN' THIS WHEN THERE'S SO MUCH I AIN'T SURE OF. LIKE WHAT THE HELL HAPPENED TO MY EYE? WHY CAN'T I REMEMBER ANYTHING AFTER THE PLANE?

AN' HOW COME I GOT FUCKED SO BAD, BY THE PEOPLE I LOVED THE MOST?

I JUST DUNNO HOW TO FIT IT IN MY HEAD.

CASS, GODDAMMIT, I SAVED HIS ASS AN' HE SAVED MINE TWICE EACH, EASY--HOW THE HELL'D HE DO SOMETHIN' LIKE THAT? HE'DA BURNED UP LIKE A FUCKIN' CRISPY CRITTER, I HADN'T STOPPED HIM...

AN' TULIP, JESUS, TULIP... I DON'T EVEN WANNA THINK...

I FEEL LIKE PUKIN'. SWEAR TO GOD.

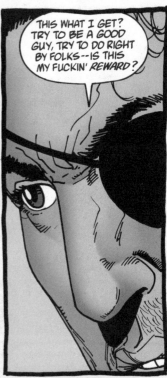

THIS WHAT I GET? TRY TO BE A GOOD GUY, TRY TO DO RIGHT BY FOLKS--IS THIS MY FUCKIN' REWARD?

WELL NOW, PILGRIM... I DON'T RECALL NOBODY SAYIN' NOTHIN' ABOUT NO REE-WARD.

POINT.

AW, FUCK THIS SELF-PITYIN' BULLSHIT.

I DUNNO.

COULD BE ALL I NEED'S TO SHIFT DOWN A GEAR.

HOW COME THERE AIN'T NO SWIMMIN' POOLS IN MEXICO? 'CAUSE ANYONE CAN SWIM'S ALREADY OVER HERE ANYHOW!

HAW! 'KAY, HOW COME MEXICANS EAT REFRIED BEANS?

'CAUSE THEY COULDN'T GET 'EM RIGHT THE FIRST TIME!

HA HA HA!

WELL, HOW 'BOUT THIS ONE--

THAT BOY GONNA SIT THERE AN' TAKE THAT?

HECTOR? SURE.

THEY RAG ON HIM FROM TIME TO TIME, JUST TO REMIND HIM OF HIS PLACE. HE SMILES AT THEIR JOKES, HE GETS TO HANG OUT WITH THEM.

FUN BUNCH LIKE THAT, I GUESS IT'S WORTH THE ABUSE...

DON'T KNOCK IT. HECTOR'S A LITTLE SLOW, DOESN'T KNOW TOO MANY PEOPLE. AND THOSE DICKS ARE PRETTY GOOD TO HIM, MOST OF THE TIME.

HELL, SOMETIMES IT'S EVEN HIS TURN TO GO HOME WITH CORA.

HAAAWWW!

LUCKY DOG.

NICE LIGHTER, STRANGER--MM--

THEY'RE HARMLESS. THEY WENT TO HIGH SCHOOL TOGETHER, DRIFTED AWAY, REALIZED THEY DIDN'T KNOW SHIT ABOUT SHIT AND DRIFTED BACK. NEVER UNDERESTIMATE THE STRANGELY MAGNETIC PULL OF THE TOWN OF SALVATION, ESPECIALLY TO THOSE AS IGNORANT AS SIN.

MOST NIGHTS, CORA TAKES HOME WHICHEVER ONE TREATS HER NICEST. I ACTUALLY THINK IT'S KIND OF SWEET.

I SWEAR. TEXAS, HUH?

YOU MEAN HECTOR? SHIT, AROUND HERE, THAT'S PROGRESS. HE WAS BLACK HE WOULDN'T EVEN BE IN HERE.

FUCK COMMUNISM

YOU DON'T MEAN--

NO, OF COURSE I FUCKING DON'T MEAN. BUT THEY WON'T COME IN. THEY CHOOSE NOT TO, THEY HAVE THEIR OWN PLACES.

COLORED FOLKS MOSTLY LIVE ON THE WEST SIDE, PLACE CALLED JOHN'S HOLLOW.

WELL, USUALLY CALLED COONTOWN. NOT BY ME, BUT ASK ANYONE ELSE FOR DIRECTIONS TO THE HOLLOW AND YOU'LL PROBABLY GET A BLANK STARE.

BUT NOT YOU.

I PREFER TO JUDGE PEOPLE BY WHAT'S IN THEM, NOT HOW THEY LOOK.

MY HALO'S IN THE MAIL, IN CASE YOU WERE WONDERING.

HOWDY.

EVENIN'.

I WAS WONDERIN' IF I COULD JOIN YOU FOR A MOMENT?

SURE.

YOU'RE THE SHERIFF, AIN'T YOU?

THAT I AM. JIM BEWLEY'S THE NAME.

JESSE CUSTER.

RIGHT. WELL, MISTER CUSTER...AH... WHAT IT IS, I SAW THAT LITTLE SET-TO YOU HAD WITH THEM BOYS TODAY? IN THE STREET?

YOU COME TO TAKE ME IN?

NO...! NO, NOT AT ALL.

MATTER OF FACT, I GOT A KINDA PROPOSITION FOR YOU.

...SO YOU SEE EVEN FOR A, A NORMALLY PEACEFUL LITTLE TOWN LIKE SALVATION, WE DO HAVE SOME PUBLIC ORDER PROBLEMS...

NAME I KEEP HEARIN' IS QUINCANNON.

OOOHH, NO, MISTER CUSTER. LEMME MAKE IT REAL CLEAR THAT MISTER QUINCANNON IS A RESPECTED BUSINESSMAN, A GENUINE OL' FASHIONED GENTLEMAN. THAT PLANT OF HIS HAS BROUGHT A LOT OF MONEY INTO THE COUNTY, A LOT OF JOBS...

BUT, TRUTH TO TELL, SOME OF THE MEN HE'S HIRED IN DO LEAVE A LITTLE TO BE DESIRED. AND THAT'S WHERE WE GET THEM PUBLIC ORDER PROBLEMS I MENTIONED.

SEE, THE TROUBLE IS, THERE'S REALLY ONLY ME TO KEEP A LID ON THINGS, YOU KNOW? AN' WELL, I AIN'T AS SPRIGHTLY AS I ONCE WAS--

DIDN'T I SEE YOU HAD A DEPUTY WITH YOU THIS AFTERNOON?

CINDY?

HELL, MISTER CUSTER, SHE'S REALLY ONLY THERE TO KEEP THE LOCAL NIGRAS HAPPY...WE GOTTA BE SEEN TO BE IMPARTIAL--IF YOU GET MY DRIFT?

EVER HAVE ANY KLAN TROUBLE ROUND HERE, SHERIFF?

DAMN, NO!

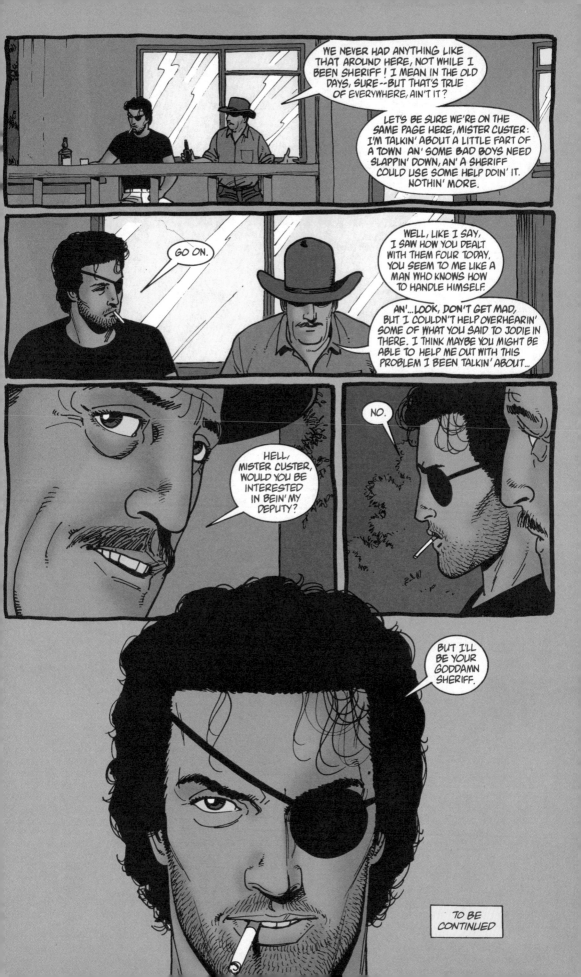

NOW...

SAY THE NAME...

SAY THE NAME

...MORNIN', BOYS.

MORNIN', MISTER QUINCANNON.

THE MEATMAN COMETH

GARTH ENNIS-Writer STEVE DILLON-Artist

Pamela Rambo-Colorist, Clem Robins-Letterer, Axel Alonso-Editor

PREACHER created by Garth Ennis and Steve Dillon

CONGRATULATIONS ON YOUR APPOINTMENT, SHERIFF CUSTER. YOU HAVE A NICE DAY.

ALREADY? AIN'T THERE GONNA BE A ELECTION?

OH, I'M SURE THEY'LL GET AROUND TO IT EVENTUALLY. THEY DID WITH ME.

NOW, HERE WE ARE... OFFICE, CRUISER, GUN-RACK, FILE CABINET...

YOU'RE HANDIN' THE WHOLE THING OVER TO ME HERE AN' NOW?

SURE AM. CINDY'S GONNA FILL YOU IN ON ALL THE DETAILS.

RELAX. FOLKS AROUND HERE AIN'T TOO CONCERNED WITH THE NICETIES, 'LONG AS YOU DO THE JOB RIGHT.

YOU KNOW, I WAS A LITTLE BIT THROWN WHEN YOU SUGGESTED THIS. BUT THE MORE I THOUGHT ABOUT IT, THE MORE I FIGURED--HELL, WHY NOT? WHY MAKE HIM A DEPUTY WHEN HE'S MORE'N HAPPY TO DO YOUR JOB?

I RECKON YOU'LL BE JUST FINE, SHERIFF.

'BYE NOW.

MM.

'BYE.

WUFF!

RECKON SO, HUH?

ME TOO.

GOOD MORNING, SHERIFF.

HUH? OH, MORNIN'.

MY OH MY...! DIDN'T TAKE YOU LONG, DID IT?

IMPECCABLE REFERENCES. YOU KNOW HOW IT IS.

TRADITION DEMANDS YOU START CLEANING THIS PLACE UP. RUN THE BAD GUYS OUT OF TOWN ON A RAIL, FALL IN LOVE WITH THE TOWN BEAUTY, ACQUIRE A DRUNKEN BUT AMUSING SIDEKICK.

HOW ABOUT IT, STRANGER?

THAT'S SHERIFF STRANGER TO YOU.

SEE YOU LATER, JODIE.

YOU MUST BE CINDY...

DEPUTY DAGGETT. YOUR OFFICE IS THROUGH HERE.

SHERIFF

WELL I'M--

I KNOW WHO YOU ARE.

I WAS HOPIN' YOU MIGHT DRIVE ME 'ROUND A LITTLE BIT LATER ON. SHOW ME THE AREA. INTRODUCE ME TO FOLKS.

I'VE GOT ALL THIS TO GET THROUGH. MAYBE THE DAY AFTER TOMORROW.

AIN'T WE GOT A SECRETARY FOR THAT?

NO. WE'VE GOT ME. APPARENTLY.

WELL THAT'S NO GOOD. YOU'RE A LAW OFFICER, YOU AIN'T GOT TIME FOR THIS BULLSHIT.

HIRE A SECRETARY. TAKE IT OUTTA MY SALARY.

MIND IF I SMOKE?

UH...NO...

YOU TWO WAIT HERE WITH THE CAR.

YESSIR.

SHERIFF

...SO OUR JURISDICTION RUNS AS FAR AS THE RIVER HERE, AN' THEN OUT TO THE COUNTY LINE HERE. IT AIN'T MUCH TO SPEAK OF.

NOPE...

SHERIFF CUSTER?

ODIN QUINCANNON.

WHY DON'T YOU HAVE YOUR GIRL HERE MAKE SOME COFFEE, AN' ME AN' YOU CAN HAVE A LITTLE TALK?

EVER HEARDA KNOCKIN'?

HEH! ONCE.

WAAAAKK--!

JESUS CHRIST!

SON OF A BITCH, HE'S SEVENTY-FIVE YEARS OLD!

THAT'S OKAY--

I HIT YOUNG FUCKS TOO--

SHIT--

WHAT THE FUCK--

I AM MR. QUINCANNON'S LAWYER AND I CAN *ASSURE YOU*, SHERIFF, THAT YOU HAVE MADE THE BIGGEST MISTAKE OF YOUR SHORT AND POINTLESS CAREER!

THIS *OUTRAGE* OF YOURS IS AN ABUSE OF POLICE AUTHORITY OUTSTRIPPING THE *KING BEATING*, AND FOR IT I INTEND TO *HOUND YOU* THROUGH EVERY--

NO!!

HE'S *MINE!* MINE! AN' WE'RE GONNA DO HIM *MY WAY!*

SIR, YOU REALLY SHOULDN'T SAY THOSE THINGS--

SHUT UP, DAMN YOU! ODIN QUINCANNON SAYS WHAT HE *LIKES!*

YOU'RE FUCKING *DEAD*, CUSTER! YOU HEAR ME?!

YEAH, YEAH, WHATEVER. YOU ASSWIPES SCRAPE THIS OL' BUZZARD UP AN' GET HIM OUTTA HERE. I DON'T WANNA SEE ANY'VE YOU IN THIS TOWN AGAIN.

FOR FUTURE REFERENCE, SHORTY: THE LAW IN SALVATION AIN'T FOR SALE NO MORE.

NOW *GIT.*

I HATE A FELLA TALKS ABOUT HIMSELF IN THE THIRD PERSON...

JODIE--MM-- I GOTTA TELL YOU, THIS IS ABOUT THE BEST DAMN CHEESEBURGER I EVER ATE...

REALLY?

UH-HUH. AN' THAT AIN'T BULL-SHIT, NEITHER. YOU'RE TALKIN' TO A BURGER CONNOISSEUR.

WELL, THANK YOU. I DO A PRETTY GOOD SZECHUAN LOBSTER STIR-FRY WITH CHILI SAUCE TOO, BUT THERE'S NOT A LOT OF CALL FOR THAT AROUND HERE.

MM.

YOU'RE QUITE A WORKER YOURSELF, AREN'T YOU, STRANGER? I SAW WHAT HAPPENED TO QUINCANNON AND HIS BOYS.

SHORT SHARP SHOCK. GETS 'EM USED TO THE NEW REGIME.

ANYHOW, THEY WERE NOTHIN'. I FIGHT PUKES LIKE THAT ON MY DAYS OFF FROM KICKIN' ASS.

MM-HMM.

DO YOU MIND ME ASKING WHAT THE HELL YOU THINK YOU'RE DOING HERE, EXACTLY?

WELL...

I GUESS YOU COULD SAY I GOT THIS JOB I GOTTA DO. AN'...UP 'TIL RECENTLY ANYHOW, IT LOOKED LIKE I WAS MAKIN' SOME PROGRESS ON IT.

THEN *BAM*-- WHOLE MESS GOES TITS-UP ON ME. ALL OF A SUDDEN I CAN'T TELL WHO'S RIGHT AND WHO'S WRONG, WHO I CAN COUNT OH, HELL, JUST ABOUT EVERYTHING DOWN TO THE WAY THE GODDAMN WORLD WORKS. AN' THAT'S SOMETHIN' I USED TO THINK I WAS *SURE OF.*

SO UNTIL I FIGURE ALL THAT OUT AN' COME UP WITH SOME ANSWERS SATISFY ME, THAT JOB'S GONNA HAVE TO STAY UNDONE.

THAT ISN'T REALLY WHAT I ASKED...

NO. WELL, LET'S JUST SAY I SAW A OPPORTUNITY TO MAKE MYSELF USEFUL 'TIL I COME UP WITH THEM ANSWERS.

I SEE. AND IS THIS HOW YOU USUALLY KILL TIME, STRANGER?

HMH.

WOULDN'T WANT FOLKS THINKIN' I WAS SOME KINDA FREELOADER NOW, WOULD I?

AN' YOU CAN CALL ME JESSE.

OH, I THINK I LIKE STRANGER JUST FINE.

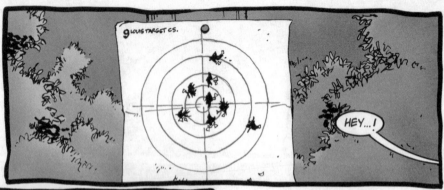

HEY...!

PRACTICE, IS ALL. YOU SHOOT MUCH?

NO, BUT I KNOW 'BOUT GOOD SHOOTIN'...SO WHAT WAS HIS DEAL WITH QUINCANNON, EXACTLY?

JUST TO IGNORE THE PLANT WORKERS WHEN THEY CAUSE TROUBLE IN TOWN, WHICH THEY DO PLENTY OF. MAKE SURE THEY DON'T HAVE TO GO TO COURT. THEY AIN'T EVEN LOCAL, THEY MOVED DOWN FROM HOUSTON, MOST'VE 'EM...

ALL BEWLEY HAD TO DO WAS LOOK THE OTHER WAY--WHICH WAS GOOD, 'CAUSE THAT'S ALL FOLKS IN SALVATION EVER DO, REALLY.

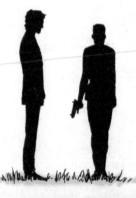

YEAH?

IT'S JUST THAT KINDA PLACE. YOU AIN'T LEFT BY THE TIME YOU'RE TWENTY-FIVE, YOU'RE STUCK.

YOU LET YOURSELF GET STUCK, YOU'RE PROBABLY THE KINDA PERSON'LL LOOK THE OTHER WAY IF IT MAKES LIFE EASIER ON YOU.

THAT INCLUDE YOU, DEPUTY DAGGETT?

OH, YOU CAN CALL ME CINDY.

IF YOU LIKE.

WANT TO TRY?

DAMN, IT'S BEEN A WHILE...

YOU'LL BE OKAY. NO, I WANTED TO LEAVE, I REALLY DID...

BUT JUST WHEN I WAS ALL SET TO GO IN THE ARMY, MY MOMMA GOT DRUNK AN' BROKE HER BACK FALLIN' OFF THE PORCH. POPS IS DEAD, MY BIG SIS KIM'S MARRIED--THAT SORTA PUT ME BEHIND THE EIGHTBALL.

I LOOK AFTER MOMMA MOST'VE THE TIME. KIM COMES OVER WHEN I'M ON DUTY, WHICH AIN'T TOO OFTEN. BEWLEY DIDN'T EVEN NEED A DEPUTY--I'M ONLY HERE 'CAUSE--

HE TOLD ME. FUCK HIM.

I NEED A DEPUTY, CINDY. I AIN'T TOO HOT AT LOOKIN' THE OTHER WAY.

YEAH...I WAS GOIN' TO ASK, DO YOU HAVE A LOT OF EXPERIENCE IN LAW ENFORCEMENT?

GRAND THEFT AUTO. NEVER GOT CAUGHT.

WHAT?

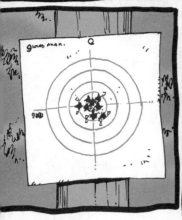

...JESUS CHRIST, WHO THE HELL TAUGHT YOU TO SHOOT?

SADISTIC FUCKIN' MADMAN I USED TO KNOW.

LONG STORY.

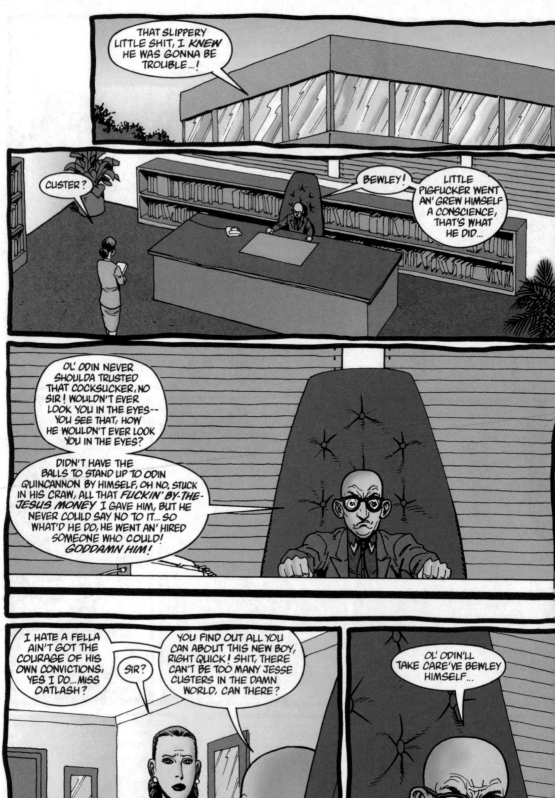

THAT SLIPPERY LITTLE SHIT, I *KNEW* HE WAS GONNA BE TROUBLE...!

CUSTER?

BEWLEY!

LITTLE PIGFUCKER WENT AN' GREW HIMSELF A CONSCIENCE, THAT'S WHAT HE DID...

OL' ODIN NEVER SHOULDA TRUSTED THAT COCKSUCKER, NO SIR! WOULDN'T EVER LOOK YOU IN THE EYES-- YOU SEE THAT, HOW HE WOULDN'T EVER LOOK YOU IN THE EYES?

DIDN'T HAVE THE BALLS TO STAND UP TO ODIN QUINCANNON BY HIMSELF, OH NO, STUCK IN HIS CRAW, ALL THAT *FUCKIN' BY-THE-JESUS MONEY* I GAVE HIM, BUT HE NEVER COULD SAY NO TO IT... SO WHAT'D HE DO, HE WENT AN' HIRED SOMEONE WHO COULD! *GODDAMN HIM!*

I HATE A FELLA AIN'T GOT THE COURAGE OF HIS OWN CONVICTIONS, YES I DO...MISS OATLASH?

SIR?

YOU FIND OUT ALL YOU CAN ABOUT THIS NEW BOY, RIGHT QUICK! SHIT, THERE CAN'T BE TOO MANY JESSE CUSTERS IN THE DAMN WORLD, CAN THERE?

OL' ODIN'LL TAKE CARE'VE BEWLEY HIMSELF...

YOU DON'T HAVE TO MOVE, JESSE. YOU'RE MORE THAN WELCOME TO STAY.

THANKS, LORIE, BUT THERE'S A LITTLE ROOM IN BACK OF MY OFFICE. I RECKON I'LL BED DOWN THERE'N GIVE YOU TWO BACK YOUR PRIVACY.

OF COURSE, YOU'RE THE TOWN SHERIFF NOW, AREN'T YOU? WITH YOUR OSTRICH AND EVERYTHING!

MY OSTRICH...OH YEAH, RIGHT, MY OSTRICH. YEAH.

LISTEN, LORIE, SOMETHIN' I WANTED TO ASK YOU ABOUT...

MM?

WHAT'S JODIE'S STORY?

I MEAN WHO IS SHE EXACTLY, YOU KNOW? WHERE'S SHE COME FROM?

OH, WELL THAT'S QUITE A TALE...

SHE HASN'T HAD IT EASY, I'LL TELL YOU THAT. WHEN I MET HER SHE'D ONLY JUST GOTTEN OUT OF A MENTAL INSTITUTION.

SHE TOLD ME SHE WAS FOUND IN THE SWAMPS YEARS AGO, A LITTLE BIT EAST OF HERE. SHE'D LOST HER ARM AND SHE WAS RAVING, COMPLETELY CRAZY, ALL SHE KNEW WAS HER NAME. SHE WAS SHOUTING IT OVER AND OVER. "*JODIE! JODIE! JODIE!*" LIKE THAT... IT SOUNDS LIKE IT WAS AWFUL FOR HER.

SHE DOESN'T KNOW WHAT HAPPENED BEFORE THAT. OR MUCH AFTER IT, EITHER. SHE'S GOT ALL THESE GAPS, SHE STILL FORGETS THINGS-- I THINK THAT'S WHY SHE WAS IN THE INSTITUTION...

WHY DO YOU ASK, ANYWAY?

I DUNNO. I JUST CAN'T FIGURE HER, I GUESS.

I MEAN SHE SEEMS SO TOUGH, YOU KNOW? HELL, SHE IS TOUGH. BUT SHE'S GOT A LOTTA CLASS ALONG WITH IT.

SHE'S SMART, TOO. NOT JUST QUICK, BUT SOPHISTICATED. SHE SPEAKS REAL WELL, REAL REFINED-- EVEN WHEN SHE'S CUSSIN'. AN' YOU ONLY GOTTA LOOK AROUND THIS PLACE TO SEE SHE'S GOT THE KINDA TASTE COMES FROM A EDUCATED BACKGROUND.

I DUNNO, SOMETHIN' JUST DON'T ADD UP...

I'VE NEVER REALLY THOUGHT ABOUT IT, TO TELL YOU THE TRUTH. I KNOW SHE LIKES YOU, THOUGH.

SHE DOES?

MM. SHE'D NEVER SAY SO-- SHE LIKES TO KEEP UP THAT HARD, GRIM SORT OF FRONT.

BUT I CAN TELL.

HMM. EAST OF HERE, YOU SAID?

LICENSE AN' REGISTRATION, THANK YOU...

AIN'T YOU GONNA TELL ME WHAT IT IS YOU THINK I DONE?

WON'T TAKE A MOMENT.

OKAY? SEE? ONE OF THE GOOD GUYS. NOW, CAN I PLEASE GET GOIN'?

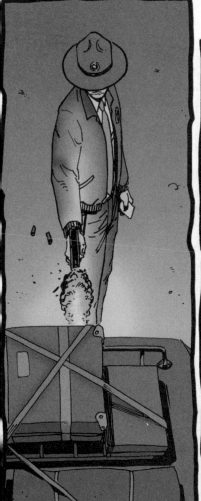

YES, SIR. DONE, SIR.

THE WHOLE TOWN'S TALKING ABOUT YOU, STRANGER. NO ONE EVER STOOD UP TO THAT LITTLE NOSEPICK QUIN-CANNON BEFORE, MUCH LESS THREW HIM THROUGH A WINDOW.

I HOPE YOU REMEMBER WHAT I SAID TO YOU ABOUT SAVING THE WORLD...

CLOSED

STRANGER?

NOT TALKING? MM? STRANGER?

WHAT ARE YOU-- ...

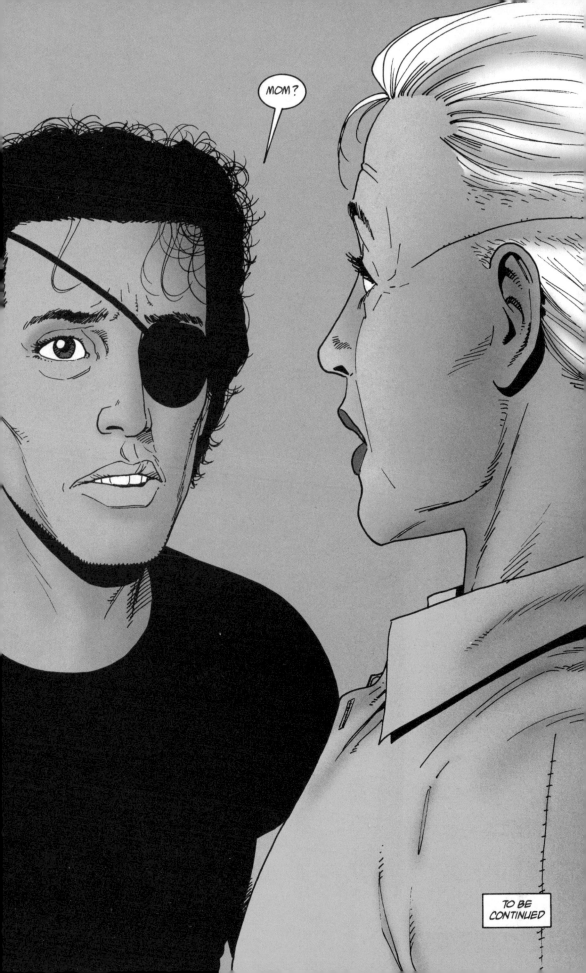

CHRISTINA'S WORLD

GARTH ENNIS-Writer STEVE DILLON-Artist

Pamela Rambo-Colorist, Clem Robins-Letterer, Axel Alonso-Editor

PREACHER created by Garth Ennis and Steve Dillon

HOW DID YOU KNOW?

DIDN'T. JUST GUESSED AN' HOPED.

THINGS YOU SAID, THINGS I SAW 'BOUT YOU. SOME STUFF LORIE TOLD ME.

YOU?

I DIDN'T EVEN IMAGINE, UNTIL YOU-- YOU CALLED ME --

OH, GOD...

JESUS.

THIS IS GOING TO TAKE SOME EXPLAINING. AND I WILL, I PROMISE I WILL.

BUT WILL YOU HOLD ME TIGHT JUST A LITTLE WHILE LONGER?

SURE, MOM.

SURE.

JESUS CHRIST...

OKAY, OKAY NOW, WE GOTTA SPREAD OUT AN' LOOK--

SHE'S HERE!

C'MON, HONEY--JESUS, FUCKIN' HELP! STOP THE GODDAMN BLEEDIN'!

OH CHRIST-- OH MY GOD--

STICK YOUR THUMB IN AN' PINCH OFF THE GODDAMN ARTERY! DO IT!

JUST THREE BOYS UP FROM HOUSTON ON A HUNTING TRIP. THEY SAVED ME. ONE OF THEM WAS AN ARMY MEDIC IN VIET-NAM, KNEW JUST WHAT TO DO...

HONEY, C'MON, YOU GOTTA STAY WITH ME NOW! DON'T GO TO SLEEP, NO, DON'T DO THAT! YOUR NAME, CAN YOU TELL ME YOUR NAME?

BILL, GET THE BOAT! OH, FUCK!

HONEY, TALK TO ME! COME ON, GODDAMMIT!!

JOOOODDYYYY!!!

I DIDN'T SPEAK AGAIN FOR TEN YEARS.

OH... FUCK...

THEY GOT ME TO A HOSPITAL, AND A SURGEON STITCHED ME UP, AND THE POLICE CAME TO ASK ME SOME QUESTIONS, AND EVENTUALLY A SHRINK TOOK A LOOK AT ME, AND NOT ONE OF THEM GOT SHIT...

SO THEY STUCK ME IN THE BIN WITH THE NAME OF THE FUCKER WHO WRECKED OUR LIVES.

JODIE

YOU WANT, WE CAN LEAVE THIS...

NO.

YOU DON'T HAVE TO TIPTOE AROUND ME, JESSE. I'M NOT WEAK AND I DON'T NEED TO BE PROTECTED. I'VE HAD FIFTY YEARS OF DEMONS TO TEACH ME THAT.

THE ASYLUM WAS IN LONGVIEW. NOBODY CAME TO SEE ME--HELL, NOBODY KNEW ME. PEOPLE WERE JUST BLANKS.

IT TOOK YEARS FOR MY MIND TO PUT ITSELF BACK TOGETHER JUST SO I COULD SURVIVE, DO BASIC THINGS LIKE FEED AND CLEAN MYSELF. THEY GAVE ME DRUGS TO HELP, BUT I WAS BARELY ABLE TO REBUILD MY INSTINCTS. THE REST WAS LOST.

OF COURSE, I DIDN'T NEED THE REST FOR THE STATE TO GET SHOT OF ME--

YOU GET YOUR TICKET AN' YOU GO ANYWHERE YOU WANT, HON. YOU KNOW WHERE YOU GOIN', MMM?

GOOD FOR YOU. YOU ALL GROWED UP NOW...

THEN IT HAPPENED. FOR THE VERY FIRST TIME, LIKE IT WOULD AGAIN AND AGAIN AND AGAIN ...

ONE OF THE BLANKS GOT FILLED IN.

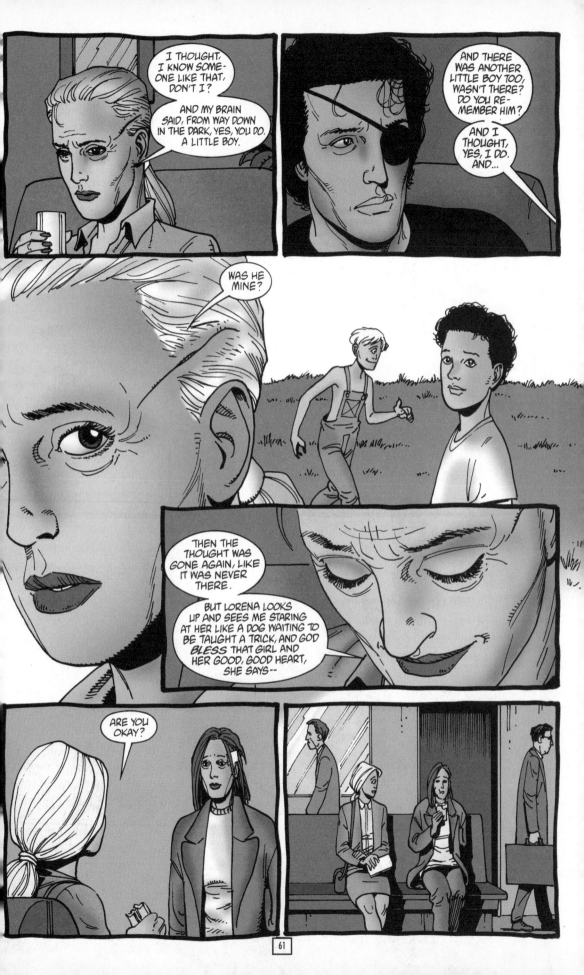

I THOUGHT, I KNOW SOMEONE LIKE THAT, DON'T I?

AND MY BRAIN SAID, FROM WAY DOWN IN THE DARK, YES, YOU DO. A LITTLE BOY.

AND THERE WAS ANOTHER LITTLE BOY TOO, WASN'T THERE? DO YOU REMEMBER HIM?

AND I THOUGHT, YES, I DO. AND...

WAS HE MINE?

THEN THE THOUGHT WAS GONE AGAIN, LIKE IT WAS NEVER THERE.

BUT LORENA LOOKS UP AND SEES ME STARING AT HER LIKE A DOG WAITING TO BE TAUGHT A TRICK, AND GOD *BLESS* THAT GIRL AND HER GOOD, GOOD HEART, SHE SAYS--

ARE YOU OKAY?

IT WAS EASIER MOVING FORWARD THAN BACK BECAUSE IT FILLED UP THE SPACES IN MY HEAD. ANYTHING NEW WAS GOOD: A HOME, A JOB, A BOOK TO READ, EVEN A GODDAMN BOTTLE OF WHISKEY. IT WAS ALL EXPERIENCE.

IT MADE ME A PERSON AGAIN.

SO I'D BE DOING SOMETHING LIKE THAT, MAYBE WORKING ON THE BAR THAT LORIE AND I WENT INTO TOGETHER--SHE PUT IN THE INHERITANCE, I PUT IN THE ATTITUDE--AND IT WOULD HAPPEN.

JODIE'S

THAT TIME WOULD COME BACK TO ME LIKE A LIGHTNING BOLT TO THE BRAIN.

JODY. THE COFFIN. THAT MORNING IN THE CORN. *HER.*

ANGELVILLE.

JESSE, I SWEAR, I *SWEAR* TO YOU--I TRIED, I TRULY DID--

MOM, I KNOW--

I'D GET ON A BUS, OR, OR A TRAIN, AND I'D BE HEADING EAST--I KNEW WHERE IT WAS, I KNEW THE FUCKING PLACE WAS--

I--I--

IT'S OKAY. SHHH.

I WAS LONG GONE BY THEN.

SHHH, NOW.

I'D BE COMING TO GET YOU AND MY FUCKING MIND WOULD GO BLANK AND I'D *FORGET ALL OVER AGAIN--!*

ALL I COULD DO WAS --COME BACK HERE--

JESUS CHRIST...!

WELL. HERE'S TO THE MAN WHO THOUGHT TO BOTTLE THIS STUFF, MM?

AMEN TO THAT.

IT WOULD BE SO STRANGE... GETTING OFF A BUS IN THE MIDDLE OF WHATEVER GODFORSAKEN HOLE I'D ENDED UP IN, WONDERING HOW, WHY, WHERE...

IT WAS EASIER MOVING FORWARD. LIKE I SAID.

SO THAT'S WHAT I RESOLVED TO DO, AND IT WORKED. THE BAD THING STOPPED COMING. I THINK I HAD MY LAST... EPISODE, MAYBE THREE OR FOUR YEARS AGO.

ALL I HAD TO DO WAS CONCENTRATE ON BEING ME.

AND THAT'S WHAT I THOUGHT I WAS DOING, WHAT I WAS SO SURE I WAS DOING, SO THAT WHEN I SAW YOU YESTERDAY IT DIDN'T EVEN CLICK.

I HEARD YOUR VOICE, I WATCHED YOU MOVE--AND YOU ARE SO LIKE YOUR FATHER THERE, JESSE, YOU WOULD NOT BELIEVE IT--I EVEN HEARD YOUR NAME...

BUT IT WASN'T 'TIL YOU WALKED IN HERE AND CALLED ME MOM--

THAT I KNEW WHO I WAS.

YOU OKAY?

A LITTLE QUEASY. EVERYTHING COMING BACK LIKE THAT, ALL THE PIECES SLAMMING INTO MY MIND AT ONCE, IT...

I DON'T KNOW. I'VE JUST REMEMBERED MY *LIFE*, JESSE.

IT THROWS YOU.

I GUESS I'M NOT WHAT YOU EXPECTED, MM?

LAST TIME I SAW YOU THAT SON OF A BITCH WAS HAULIN' YOU AWAY TO KILL YOU. I AIN'T HAD NOTHIN' TO EXPECT MY WHOLE GOD-DAMN LIFE.

YOU'RE MY MOM AN' YOU'RE ALIVE, AN' BY GOD THAT'S ALL THAT MATTERS TO ME.

OH GOD, THAT PLACE. YOU WERE...WHAT WERE YOU, TEN?

THAT PLACE AND THOSE MONSTERS...

AND THAT VICIOUS OLD--

THEY'RE GONE, MOM.

I WENT BACK. I KILLED 'EM.

I CHOKED THE LIFE OUTTA JODY AN' BURNED THE DAMN HOUSE DOWN. GRAN'MA WENT UP WITH IT.

THEY'RE IN HELL.

GOOD BOY.

GOOD BOY.

SAY, YOU KNOW WHAT? I SAW THE PICTURE.

MM?

THE WYETH. YOU REMEMBER.

THEY GOT THE ORIGINAL IN THE MUSEUM OF MODERN ART IN NEW YORK.

YOU SAW IT?

uh-huh.

WHAT WAS IT LIKE...?

IT WAS BEAUTIFUL, MOM. COLORS WERE SO VIVID, MORE'N ANY BOOK OR PRINT COULD REPRODUCE.

IT WAS ABOUT THE SADDEST THING I EVER DID SEE.

SO YOU REMEMBERED.

YOU USED TO STARE AT IT FOR HOURS, BUT I NEVER DID KNOW WHY AT THE TIME. WASN'T 'TIL THE MUSEUM I FIGURED IT OUT.

I FOUND IT IN A BOOK IN THAT HUGE LIBRARY IN ANGELVILLE. I WAS ABOUT TWELVE, JUST STARTING TO UNDERSTAND THAT THINGS WOULD NEVER CHANGE FOR ME...AND I READ ABOUT THE PICTURE...

AND MY GOD, I THOUGHT, MY GOD.

SOMEBODY'S PAINTED MY LIFE.

CHRISTINA'S WORLD

THE GIRL WAS SOME COUSIN OF WYETH'S. SHE HAD POLIO.

I KNOW, MOM.

SHE WAS SO WEAK, AND THIS WAS AS FAR AS SHE COULD GO, THE BOTTOM OF THE FIELD. ALWAYS IN VIEW OF THE HOUSE.

I REMEMBER.

IT CENTERED HER WORLD. SHE COULDN'T ESCAPE IT. IT REACHED OUT AND BROUGHT HER BACK, NO MATTER WHAT...

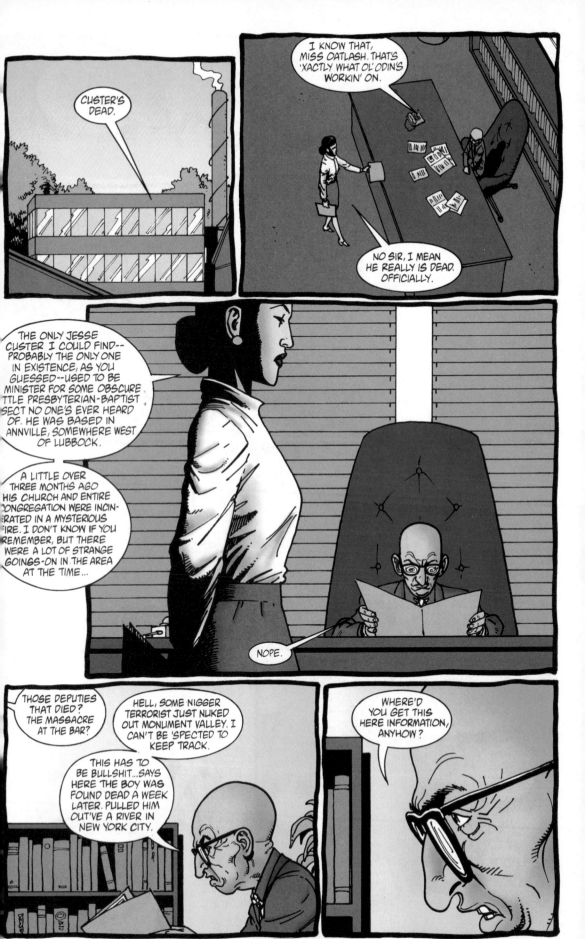

AN ASSOCIATE OF MINE, SIR. HE WORKS FOR THE BUREAU, IN THEIR RECORDS DIVISION. HE SAYS THEY'VE OFFICIALLY CLOSED THE CASE.

ASSOCIATE? WENT TO GODDAMN YALE TOGETHER, YOU MEAN! S'POSE THAT'S WHERE YOU KNOW HIM FROM!

OL' ODIN NEVER HAD NO FANCY EDUCATION, NO SIR! ODIN QUINCANNON STARTED OUT SO POOR HE HAD TO WIPE HIS ASS WITH HIS HAND!

BUT HE PULLED HIMSELF UP BY HIS BOOTSTRAPS AN' MADE SOMETHIN' OF HIS LIFE, AN' BY GOD HE DID IT ALONE! ODIN CLEANS HIS CRACK WITH SMOOTHEST SILK TODAY; AN' HE DIDN'T GET THERE BY EXPLOITIN' CONTACTS AN' CALLIN' IN FAVORS FROM NO FAGGY FUCKIN' LAW SCHOOL! HE GOT THERE BY HARD FUCKIN' WORK!

WE DIDN'T ATTEND LAW SCHOOL TOGETHER, SIR. WE USED TO COMMIT ACTS OF EXTREME SEXUAL DEVIANCY TOGETHER IN A MOTEL ROOM IN AUSTIN, INCLUDING BONDAGE AND GOLDEN SHOWERS.

THAT'S WHERE I KNOW HIM FROM.

OH. WELL. SO CUSTER'S OFFICIALLY DEAD, HUH? GOT NO KIN, NO PAST WORTH TALKIN' ABOUT...

THAT'S CORRECT, MR. QUIN- CANNON.

WELL, I GUESS THERE AIN'T NOBODY GONNA MISS HIM THEN, IS THERE?

JODIE'S B

YOU FIXIN' TO LEAVE THE SIGN LIKE THAT?

OH, I DON'T KNOW. I WAS JODIE FOR NEARLY TWENTY YEARS. NO POINT TRYING TO DENY IT.

SO WHAT NEXT?

NEXT IS GETTING TO KNOW YOU AGAIN, I HOPE. IF YOU'RE GOING TO BE AROUND.

I'LL BE HERE.

THIS THING I STARTED WITH QUINCANNON, I CAN'T RIGHTLY LEAVE TILL IT'S OVER AN' DONE WITH. AIN'T NO WAY THE LITTLE BASTARD'LL LET IT GO ANYWAY.

SAVING THE WORLD?

DOIN' WHAT'S RIGHT.

AH, GOOD EVENING, SHERIFF.

EVENIN'...

AND LORENA TELLS ME IT IS NOW CHRISTINA, IS THAT RIGHT?

LONG STORY, GUNTHER.

TIME TO GO HOME, I THINK.

MM? OH, HEY THERE...

YES, YOUR MOTHER IS CLOSING UP FOR THE NIGHT.

MIGHT I TROUBLE YOU FOR A LIGHT, SHERIFF?

SURE.

THANK YOU--MM--

NO PROBLEM. SO I UNDERSTAND YOU CAME FROM GERMANY, THAT RIGHT? THAT BE AFTER THE WAR?

MORE OR LESS, YES.

AS A MATTER OF FACT, PERHAPS YOU HAD BETTER ARREST ME. I CAME HERE TO SPY FOR THE NAZIS IN WORLD WAR TWO.

HEH.

NO, SERIOUSLY.

GOODNIGHT, SHERIFF CUSTER.

TO BE CONTINUED

LET'S GO, DEPUTY.

WUFF!

WELL, FIRST WE GONNA DRIVE OVER TO JOHN'S HOLLOW AN' PICK UP CINDY, AN' THEN WE GONNA GO MEET SOME FOLKS. KINDA GET TO KNOW THE TOWN A LITTLE BIT.

WUFF! WUFF!

THEN WE GONNA PICK UP SOME GROCERIES AN' SUCH, AN' SWING BY MOM'S IN TIME FOR LUNCH. HOW'S THAT SOUND?

...MOM'S. I SWEAR.

GODDAMMIT...

FIRST WE GONNA CALL CINDY AN' HAVE HER BRING OVER THE CRUISER. THEN WE GONNA TAKE A SLEDGEHAMMER TO THIS WORN-OUT PIECE OF SHIT.

THEN WE GONNA GO GRAB A BEER. HOW'S *THAT* SOUND?

CUSTER'S LAW

GARTH ENNIS - Writer STEVE DILLON - Artist

Pamela Rambo - Colorist, Clem Robins - Letterer, Axel Alonso - Editor

PREACHER created by Garth Ennis and Steve Dillon

YOU COME UP TO ODIN'S OFFICE RIGHT QUICK, HEAR?

THAT RETARD I HIRED FUCKED UP! DAMN BOMB WENT OFF WHEN CUSTER WASN'T EVEN IN THE DAMN TRUCK!

MR. QUINCANNON--!

MISS OATLASH!

SIR?

I KEEP TELLING YOU, I CANNOT BE PARTY TO ANY SUCH ACTIVITY! I AM A RESPECTED ATTORNEY AT LAW-- I CAN'T DISCUSS *BOMBING PEOPLE* OVER THE TELEPHONE!

WELL GET ON OVER HERE AN' DISCUSS IT, THEN!

KRAKAAOOWW!

MISS OATLASH...I THINK YOU'RE UP TO YOUR DAMN FUN AN' GAMES AGAIN AN' I *TOLD* YOU, I CAN'T AFFORD NO MORE WORKERS REPORTIN' SICK...

IT IS A PRIVATE ARRANGEMENT BETWEEN MYSELF AND THE MEN, MR. QUINCANNON.

IF THEIR PHYSICAL CONDITION IS DETERIORATING AS A RESULT, THEN THEY SHOULDN'T--

KRAK AAAOOOW!

TAKE--

KRAK EEEIIGGHH!

MY--

KRAK NOOO!!

MONEY!!

KRAK AAAIIEE!

THIS IS PRIVATE PRUUCCHH

JESSE--

WHERE'S QUINCANNON?

WHAT-- WHO--YOU CAN'T--

TELL ME.

DEMOLITION EXPERIENCE MY ASS, THAT GODDAMN HILL-BILLY COULDN'T CHANGE THE BATTERIES ON HIS OLD LADY'S VIBRATOR...

WHAT'S THAT COMMOTION DOWNSTAIRS?

M-M-MR. QUINCANNON?

WHAT THE HELL WAS *THAT*?!

OL' INJUN TRICK.

I JUST COULDN'T STOP HIM, SIR, HE-- IT WAS LIKE--SIR, I'M SORRY, HE'S COMING UP--

WHO IS?!

OH FUCK--

C'MERE, YOU LITTLE PECKERHEAD--

NO! GET OUT! YOU STAY AWAY FROM ME, I'M WARNIN' YOU!

SHERIFF CUSTER, HOW DARE YOU! THIS IS PRIVATE PROPERTY!

SHERIFF CUSTER, I MUST WARN YOU THAT THIS ACTION CONSTITUTES A VIOLATION OF MR. QUINCANNON'S RIGHTS AND IS TOTALLY ILLEGAL!

I AM A WITNESS! THIS IS OUTRAGEOUS!

STOP!!

NO! NOOO! AAAAAH, MOMMY, DADDY, MAKE HIM GET OFFA ME!

OH GOD-- OH CHRIST--

HEEELLLPP!!

HOLY JESUS, STOP!

THE FUCK I WILL--

GODDAMMIT, JESSE! YOU CAN'T DO THIS!

AAAIIIEEEGH!!!

...WHY NOT?

BECAUSE IT'S *AGAINST THE LAW.*

HMMM.

GLURK--!

EXTENSIVE DAMAGE TO ONE SHERIFF'S DEPARTMENT VEHICLE, SHORTY.

GO FETCH YOUR CHECK-BOOK.

ATTABOY.

WORD OF ADVICE, LITTLE MAN: AIN'T NO ONE EVER TOOK A SHOT AT ME AN' WALKED AWAY INTACT BEFORE, 'SPECIALLY NOT NO SAWED-OFF RUNT LIKE YOU. YOU PLAY SMART AN' CALL THIS QUITS, HEAR?

AN' MISS OUTLASH?

YES?

DON'T TRY TO FRIGHTEN ME WITH THE LAW, MA'AM.

YOU AIN'T SCARY.

I, UH... I JUST GOTTA GO TO THE BATHROOM...

ME TOO.

HE AIN'T GONNA QUIT...

NO HE AIN'T. HE'S THE KIND LIKES TO TAKE CARE OF THINGS PERSONAL.

AIN'T NO SATISFACTION IN SENDIN' A MAN TO JAIL WHEN WHAT YOU REALLY WANT IS TO LOOK HIM IN THE EYES WHILE YOU'RE CHOKIN' HIM TO DEATH.

TELL YOU THE TRUTH, I CAN SORTA RELATE.

SO I NOTICED. AN' I THINK IT'S SOMETHIN' WE GONNA HAVE TO TALK ABOUT.

YEAH?

I SAW YOU IN THERE, JESSE, YOU WOULDA MURDERED THAT MAN, I HADN'T OF STOPPED YOU.

NOW I DON'T KNOW HOW YOU'RE USED TO DOIN' THINGS, BUT YOU CAN'T BE YOUR OWN EXECUTIONER HERE. ONCE YOU PUT THAT STAR ON, YOU AGREE TO ABIDE BY THE LAW AN' APPLY IT *FAIRLY AN' EQUALLY.*

YOU CAN'T JUST *KILL* ODIN QUINCANNON, EVEN IF HE IS A SON OF A BITCH. YOU CAN'T EVEN MOVE AGAINST HIM, 'LESS YOU GOT PROOF.

PROOF HE TRIED TO KILL YOU. PROOF HE'S PISSIN' ON THE RULES AROUND HERE, MESSIN' UP THE RIVER WITH FILTH FROM HIS PLANT AN' LETTIN' HIS BOYS RUN RIOT IN SALVATION. YOU ACT WITHOUT IT, HE'S GONNA WIN AN' WE'LL BE IN A WORLD OF SHIT THE SMARTEST LAWYER IN TEXAS COULDN'T GET US OUT OF...

AN' WHAT THE *HELL* WAS THAT SHIT YOU PULLED ON THE RECEPTIONIST? I SWEAR, THAT THING YOU DID WITH YOUR VOICE FELT LIKE NAILS SCRAPIN' DOWN INSIDE MY SOUL!

LOAN ME THE CRUISER TONIGHT? I GOT SOMEONE I GOTTA GO SEE.

BUY YOU LUNCH...

YEAH, BRIBERY MIGHT WORK.

IT'S JUST THE ONCE. I'LL GET ME SOME MORE TRANSPORT ONCE ODIN'S CHECK CLEARS.

HELL, YOU GOT ENOUGH FOR TWO TRUCKS HERE.

SO IS THIS YOURS OR THE DEPARTMENT'S, YOU THINK?

WELL, IT'S MADE OUT TO THE DEPARTMENT. AN' WE AIN'T GOT MUCH OF A BUDGET, AFTER ALL.

MY THOUGHTS EXACTLY. SO AS LONG AS YOU'RE SPLASHIN' OUT--

CAN I GET ONE OF THESE?

DON'T SEE WHY NOT.

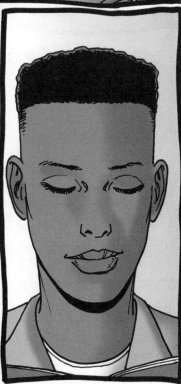

WUFF!

YOU LIKE HER, HUH?

NO GETTIN' AWAY FROM IT. SHE'S A PEACH.

SMART, TOO. GONNA TAKE SOME GETTIN' USED TO, BEIN' ON THIS SIDE'VE THE LAW.

WHICH I GUESS MEANS NO WORD OF GOD, AT LEAST FOR THE TIME BEIN'.

TRICKY ONE, SKEETER. DAMN THING'S LIKE A GUN: YOU PULL IT OUT WHEN YOU GOT NO CHOICE, FINE. YOU STICK IT IN SOME OL' RECEPTIONIST GAL'S FACE, WELL, THAT AIN'T SO GOOD.

THAT AIN'T MY STYLE.

?

NOW I WENT THROUGH SOME SHIT A WHILE BACK, BAD STUFF I CAN'T GET STRAIGHT IN MY HEAD. COULD BE IT'S MADE ME CARELESS.

AN' THE WORD... IT'S KINDA OF THAT TIME, AN' I AIN'T TOO SURE I'M READY TO GO BACK THERE JUST YET.

TRICKY.

JODIE'S B

DID YOU COMB YOUR HAIR THIS MORNING?

JODIE'S B

HUH? AW, MOM--!

JOKE.

HMH.

YOU LOOK REAL NICE.

THANK YOU. I FEEL NICE. I'VE BEEN ENJOYING MY FIRST WEEK OF BEING ME AGAIN.

Y'ALL EVER DO CROSSWORD PUZZLES?

NOT TOO OFTEN...

I THINK YOU TWO HAVE ALREADY MET. TOBY WORKS FOR ME.

SURE, DUDE. YOU SCARED THE CRAP OUTTA DAVY DREW.

SO I GOT NORTH AMERICAN BURROWIN' RODENT. SIX LETTERS.

G--

BUFFALO!

BEE-YOU-EFF-EYE-EL-OH...

89

I'VE BEEN EXPECTING YOU.

YEAH, WELL, I HEARD THERE WAS A NAZI SPY LIVIN' HERE. FIGURED IT MIGHT BE WORTH INVESTIGATIN'.

COME IN, SHERIFF.

NICE PLACE.

THANK YOU. FEEL FREE TO SMOKE.

SO...

SO, I CHECKED WITH THE RECORDS OFFICE IN THE TOWN HALL. ACCORDIN' TO THEM, THIS HOUSE BELONGS TO ONE *MARK VAN DER POL.*

HAS DONE FOR ALMOST FIFTY YEARS.

THAT NAME DON'T SOUND TOO GERMAN TO ME.

DUTCH. I STOPPED USING IT YEARS AGO. WHEN I BECAME AN AMERICAN CITIZEN I REVERTED TO MY OWN NAME, WHICH I'D BEEN USING SOCIALLY ALMOST SINCE I GOT HERE.

BUT VAN DER POL WAS THE NAME ON THE PASSPORT THAT GOT ME INTO SAN DIEGO, IN JUNE OF NINETEEN FORTY-THREE.

UH-*HUH*...

ALL OF WHICH DESERVES AN EXPLANATION.

I WAS BORN GUNTHER WILHELM HAHN IN LEIPZIG, IN THE WINTER OF NINETEEN TWENTY-THREE. MY FATHER DIED OF INFLUENZA NOT LONG AFTER, THEN MY MOTHER, OF A BROKEN HEART. WHEN I WAS TEN MY OLDER BROTHER *WERNER* JOINED THE ARMY, AND I WAS ROBBED OF MY ONE TRUE FRIEND.

I *IDOLIZED* WERNER. HE DOMINATED MY EARLY LIFE. HE WAS SOON FLYING FIGHTERS FOR THE LUFTWAFFE, WHICH IN MY EYES MADE HIM GREATER STILL.

THE DAY HE MADE ACE OVER SPAIN I FELT LIKE I WAS RELATED TO SOME GOD. THE WAY OTHER BOYS LOOKED AT ME, WERNER HAHN'S BROTHER, WELL...

HE COMMANDED A FULL SQUADRON IN THE BLITZKRIEG, AND WAS WELL ON HIS WAY TO A KNIGHT'S CROSS BY THE TIME OF THE BATTLE OF BRITAIN. *LONDON IN A MONTH*, HIS LETTER SAID.

AS YOU CAN IMAGINE, I COULD NOT WAIT TO FOLLOW IN HIS FOOTSTEPS. THAT I DID NOT IS THE REASON I AM HERE TO TALK TO YOU TONIGHT.

BECAUSE THE ENGLISH SHOT HIM FROM THE SKY ON THE VERY SAME MORNING HE SENT ME THAT LETTER.

I MET WERNER'S COMMANDING OFFICER AT THE FUNERAL.

HE WAS A KIND MAN, OBERST LIFERTZ. YES, MY BROTHER DIED BRAVELY. KILLED INSTANTLY; COULDN'T HAVE FELT A THING. I WAS JOINING THE JAGDWAFFE? EXCELLENT. HE'D PUT IN A GOOD WORD WHEN I APPLIED.

WHICH I INTENDED TO DO ON MY VERY NEXT BIRTHDAY...

BUT?

BUT, I FOUND LIFERTZ THAT NIGHT IN A BAR I SOMETIMES WENT TO, DRUNK AND BITTER AT THE LIES HE'D HAD TO TELL. LIES HE WAS TELLING WITH INCREASING FREQUENCY.

IN THE MESSERSCHMITT 109, LIFERTZ EXPLAINED, THE AUXILIARY FUEL TANK WAS BENEATH THE PILOT'S SEAT. ALL IT EVER TOOK WAS A SINGLE ROUND OF TRACER.

THEY RECKONED THAT THE FIRE WOULD RAISE THE COCKPIT TEMPERATURE FROM NORMAL TO THREE THOUSAND DEGREES IN TEN SECONDS. IF YOU WEREN'T OUT BY THEN, YOU WEREN'T GETTING OUT AT ALL.

WERNER WAS STILL SCREAMING AFTER TWENTY.

I RESOLVED THEN AND THERE THAT I WAS NOT GOING TO DIE LIKE THAT.

INSTEAD I JOINED THE LUFTWAFFE'S INTELLIGENCE DIVISION, TO WHICH I WAS MUCH BETTER SUITED.

I WAS NEVER A NATURAL WARRIOR, JESSE.

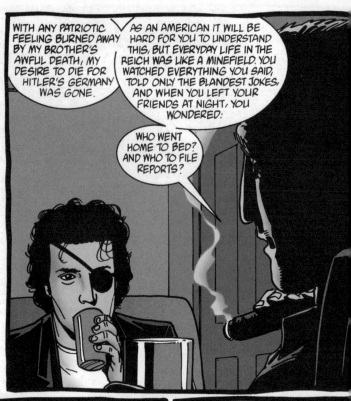WITH ANY PATRIOTIC FEELING BURNED AWAY BY MY BROTHER'S AWFUL DEATH, MY DESIRE TO DIE FOR HITLER'S GERMANY WAS GONE.

AS AN AMERICAN IT WILL BE HARD FOR YOU TO UNDERSTAND THIS, BUT EVERYDAY LIFE IN THE REICH WAS LIKE A MINEFIELD. YOU WATCHED EVERYTHING YOU SAID, TOLD ONLY THE BLANDEST JOKES, AND WHEN YOU LEFT YOUR FRIENDS AT NIGHT, YOU WONDERED:

WHO WENT HOME TO BED? AND WHO TO FILE REPORTS?

IT WAS NO WAY TO LIVE.

I GREW *SICK* OF ENDLESSLY, FEARFULLY REVIEWING MY CONVERSATIONS FOR SEDITION, AND BY THE END OF FORTY-ONE I KNEW WE WOULD LOSE ANYWAY. RUSSIA WAS ONE THING, BUT *AMERICA*...?

THINGS WOULD GET BAD, I WAS CERTAIN. I DOUBTED THERE WOULD EVEN *BE* A GERMANY ONCE THE DUST HAD SETTLED. HOW TO GET OUT, I WONDERED, HOW TO GET OUT...

GO BE A SPY IN THE STATES.

IN ONE.

I VOLUNTEERED AND WAS ACCEPTED BY THE ABWEHR. TOP MARKS ALL THE WAY THROUGH TRAINING.

"HIGHLY *MOTIVATED*," MY INSTRUCTOR WROTE. "SHOULD GO FAR."

SO MARK VAN DER POL ARRIVED IN THE UNITED STATES, A REFUGEE FROM THE DUTCH EAST INDIES WITH FIVE HUNDRED DOLLARS SEWN IN HIS OVERCOAT.

I HAD A CONTACT ARRANGED IN LOS ANGELES. I HAD NO INTENTION OF GOING ANYWHERE NEAR IT.

FOR ALL I KNOW, "CODENAME EAGLE" IS STILL SITTING IN A BAR ON HOLLYWOOD BOULEVARD, WAITING FOR A TALL DUTCHMAN IN A BLUE HAT.

NO, I WENT EAST AND LOST MYSELF IN THE WIDE OPEN SPACES. NOBODY NOTICED ONE MORE DRIFTER. THE WAR WAS A WORLD AWAY.

I SETTLED... AND IT DIDN'T TAKE ME LONG TO REALIZE THAT I ENJOYED MY NEW LIFE VERY, VERY MUCH.

HOW SO?

BECAUSE IT WAS SO MUCH BETTER THAN WHAT I WAS USED TO.

I LIKE THIS COUNTRY, JESSE. I LIKE BASEBALL AND WHISKEY AND MOM'S APPLE PIE--NOT MY MOM'S APPLE PIE, BUT YOU KNOW WHAT I MEAN--AND THE STARS AND STRIPES, AND JOHN WAYNE, AND FIREWORKS ON THE FOURTH OF JULY...

AND I LIKE THE MYTH OF THE PLACE.

THE MYTH OF AMERICA: THAT SIMPLE, HONEST MEN, BORN OF HER GREAT PLAINS AND WOODS AND SKIES HAVE MADE A NATION OF HER, AND WILL PROVE WORTHY OF HER WHEN THE TIME IS RIGHT.

UNDER HARSH LIGHT IT IS FALSE.

BUT A GOOD MYTH TO LIVE UP TO, ALL THE SAME.

SO WHY TRUST ME WITH ALL OF THIS?

THIS IS YOUR TOWN NOW, JESSE. I FELT IT RIGHT THAT YOU SHOULD KNOW.

THIS IS HOW HONORABLE MEN DEAL WITH ONE ANOTHER, IS IT NOT?

AN' YOU RECKON THAT'S THE CASE HERE?

YOUR FIRST DAY IN TOWN YOU COULD HAVE SMASHED THAT BOY'S FACE, BUT INSTEAD YOU CHOSE TO LET HIM GO. THAT WAS THE KEY. AND TAKING ON THE TASK YOU HAVE...?

MEN LIKE YOU CANNOT DISGUISE WHAT THEY ARE.

WELL, NOW...

WAY I ALWAYS SEEN IT, GUNTHER, WHAT THIS COUNTRY'S ABOUT IS A SECOND CHANCE. FELLA COMES HERE, LEAVES THE OLD WORLD BEHIND, GETS ANOTHER SHOT AT MAKIN' IT.

YOU SEEM LIKE YOU MADE THE MOST'VE YOUR SHOT, SO WHO THE HELL AM I TO TAKE IT AWAY FROM YOU?

THERE... IS THE QUESTION OF MY ILLEGAL ENTRY TO THE STATES...

LAW'S ONLY ANY USE IF IT DOES SOME GOOD.

AND IS THAT HOW YOU INTEND TO APPLY IT, SHERIFF?

... I GUESS IT IS.

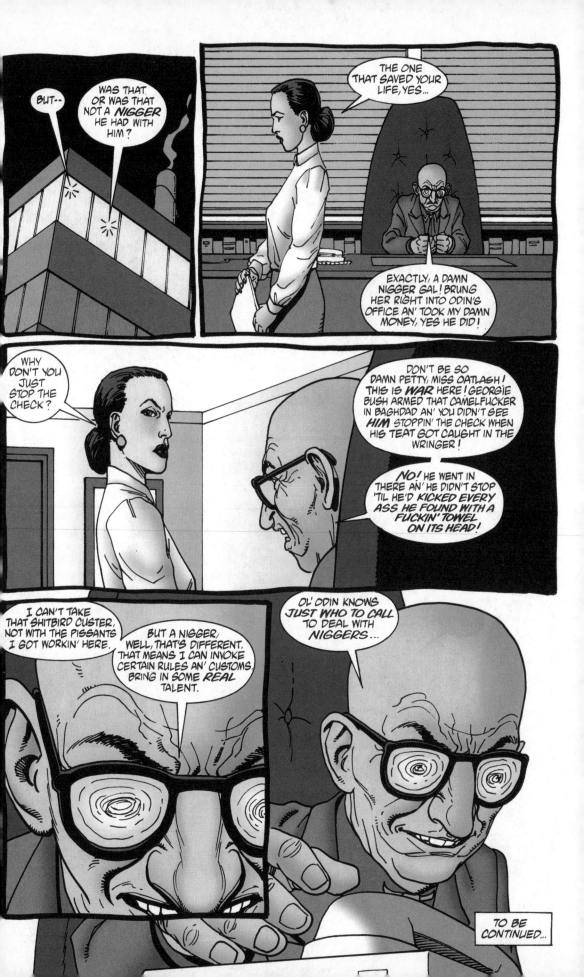

SOUTHERN CROSS

GARTH ENNIS - Writer   **STEVE DILLON - Artist**

PAMELA RAMBO - Colorist   CLEM ROBINS - Letterer   AXEL ALONSO - Editor
PREACHER created by GARTH ENNIS and STEVE DILLON

BRING OUT THE PRISONERS...

SHERIFF

QUINCANNON MEATS

WHAT ARE THE CHARGES?

MANY AN' VARIED. DISTURBIN' THE PEACE, PROPERTY DAMAGE, PUBLIC INDECENCY, ASSAULT, POSSESSION OF A OFFENSIVE WEAPON...

THEY SEEM A LITTLE THE WORSE FOR WEAR.

...RESISTIN' ARREST...

OH, AN' THIS'N FUCKED THAT'N IN THE CELLS. BUT I GUESS THAT'S THEIR BUSINESS.

RIGHT UP THE DAMN ASS...

I COME TO THIS TOWN TO GET LAID AN' BY GOD I WASN'T GOIN' HOME 'TIL I DID. YOU HADN'T OF LOCKED US UP, I WOULDN'T OF HAD TO SETTLE FOR BILLY...

UP THE ASS, SWEET JESUS.

AN' CELLS, WHO THE FUCK ARE YOU TRYNNA KID! THAT AIN'T NO CELL DOWN THERE, THAT AIN'T NOTHIN' BUT A GODDAMN STINKIN' OL' FRUIT CELLAR!

SHERIFF CUSTER, I NEED HARDLY REMIND YOU OF THE LAWS CONCERNING THE DETENTION OF PRISONERS IN HUMANE CONDITIONS...

I CAUGHT THIS DRUNK PIECE OF SHIT PISSIN' IN A FELLA'S MAILBOX. DON'T TALK TO ME 'BOUT HUMANE CONDITIONS.

NOW, YOU WANNA PUT UP THE BAIL FOR THESE FUCKS, YOU KNOW THE ROUTINE. SIGN THE FORM, LEAVE THE CHECK, GET 'EM OUTTA HERE AN' HAVE EVERY WORTHLESS ONE'VE 'EM IN FRONTA THE JUDGE MONDAY MORNIN'.

BOYS.

RIGHT, GET ON THE TRUCK...

THIRD TIME IN TWO WEEKS, MISS OATLASH. AIN'T YOU GOT TIREDA THIS YET?

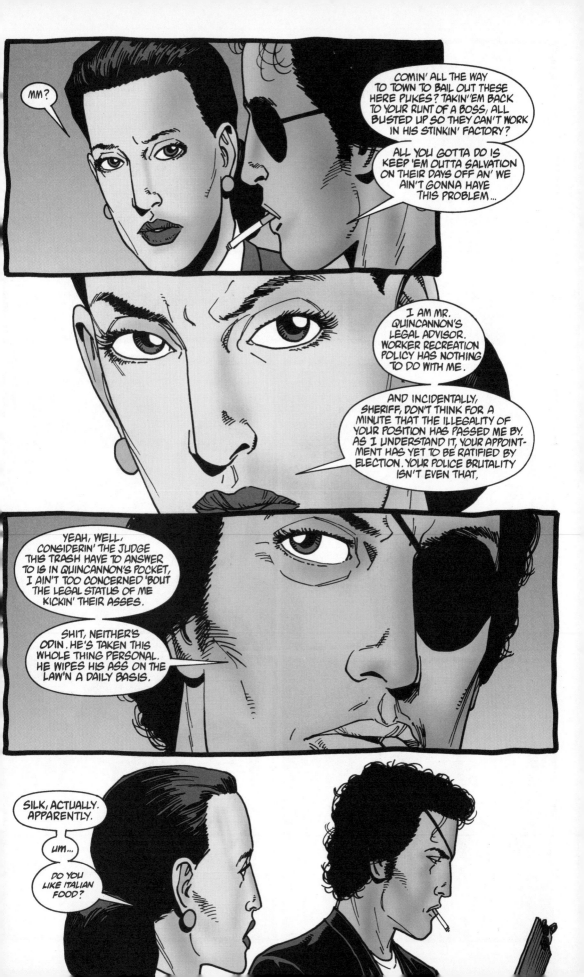

WHAT?

NOTHING!

...NOTHING.

'KAY. NOW, YOU GOT YOUR TRUCK-LOADA SCUM AN' YOUR RECEIPT, SO YOU'RE ALL THROUGH. TAKE THE PUNCHBAG TWINS AN' GO HOME.

Y'ALL STILL HERE?

AND THAT'S THE NEW SHERIFF'S DEPARTMENT OFFICIAL TRANSPORT, IS IT?

AW, I STILL HAD A CHUNKA CHANGE LEFT OVER AFTER I MAILED JOHNNY-LEE BACK HIS MONEY. AN' HELL, WAY I FIGURED, ONLY THING MORE QUINTESSENTIALLY AMERICAN THAN ONE'VE THESE'D BE A GODDAMN HORSE...

YOU ARE JUST LIKE YOUR FATHER, JESSE.

LIVING A WESTERN.

AM I REALLY LIKE HIM, MOM?

OH YES.

YOU HAVE A SENSE OF PURPOSE DRIVING YOU TO DO WHAT YOU FEEL YOU MUST. A STRONG ONE, LIKE A FIRE INSIDE YOU.

IN JOHN IT HAD ABATED. VIETNAM DID THAT. IT HADN'T BURNT OUT, BUT HE'D MADE HIS PEACE WITH IT.

I HOPE YOU CAN.

AFTER YOU, SIR.

WUFF.

GOOD MEN WITH ENGINES, TOO.

BUT THAT DIDN'T COME FROM HIM, DID IT?

I GUESS NOT.

THAT WAS JODY.

CREDIT WHERE CREDIT'S DUE, HE TAUGHT YOU WELL.

HE SURE DID. AN' MORE'N JUST ENGINES. HORSES. HUNTIN' AN' SHOOTIN'.

SHOWED ME HOW TO FIGHT LIKE A SON OF A BITCH, HELL, I DOUBT I COULDA HAD A BETTER TEACHER FOR THAT...

YOU STRANGLED HIM, RIGHT?

'TIL HIS GODDAMN EYES BUGGED OUT.

SEE YOU LATER, MOM.

BOYS, BOYS, I UNDERSTAND HOW YOU FEEL...

THEN HOW COME YOU AIN'T DONE NOTHIN' ABOUT IT?

THAT MOTHER-FUCKER CUSTER'S PUT SIX'VE OUR GUYS IN THE INFIRMARY SINCE HE STARTED, AN' THE DOC SAYS BIG JIM'S BALLS ARE RECEDED FOR GOOD!

NOW YOU *KNOW* THE ONLY REASON YOU GOT US TO MOVE TO THIS HERE SHIT-HOLE WAS YOU PROMISED US THE RUN OF THAT TOWN FOR LETTIN' OFF STEAM! AN' THAT MEANS DRINKIN' AN' WHORIN' AN' DOIN' AS WE PLEASE, NOT GET-TIN' WHIPPED AN' JAILED AN' ENDIN' UP HAVIN' TO FUCK BILLY!

UP THE ASS, NO LESS.

BOYS, IF YOU'LL JUST LEAVE THINGS IN MY CAPABLE HANDS--

YOU AIN'T JERKIN' ME OFF. THAT'S WORSE'N FUCKIN' BILLY.

I SWEAR. UP THE ASS.

NO--I MEANT--

SAY! WHY DON'T WE JUST ALL GO BACK DOWN THERE AN' GET THE SON OF A BITCH FOR KICKIN' OUR ASSES?

BECAUSE HE'D KICK YOUR ASSES AGAIN, YOU IGNORANT REDNECK.

OH YEAH...

LOOK, BOYS, OL' ODIN'S GOT IT ALL UNDER CONTROL. YOU GO ON BACK TO WORK. THIS TIME NEXT WEEK CUSTER'S GONNA SEEM NO MORE'N A BAD MEMORY, AN' SALVATION'LL BE YOURS AGAIN.

YOU GOT MY WORD ON THAT.

I HOPE SO, QUINCANNON. 'CAUSE YOU DON'T FIX THIS THING, WE AIN'T STICKIN' ROUND HERE TO WADE IN BLOOD AN' COW-SHIT AN' SLICE UP THEM STINKIN' BEASTS OF YOURS. WE GONNA BE BACK IN HOUSTON FASTER'N A MINNOW SWIMMIN' A DIPPER.

YOU TWO ASSHOLES?

SIR?

THERE'S SOME BOYS ARRIVIN' AROUND FOUR THIS AFTERNOON. YOU SEE TO IT THEY AIN'T DELAYED BY SECURITY OR ANY'VE THAT BULLSHIT.

AND MISS OATLASH, YOU LET MY SECRETARY KNOW THEY AIN'T TO BE KEPT WAITIN'. SEND 'EM RIGHT IN.

TILL THEN ODIN AIN'T TO BE DISTURBED. NOT FOR ANYTHIN', UNDERSTAND?

YESSIR.

GOOD.

NOW LEMME SEE IF I GOT THIS STRAIGHT...

YOU, WALTER, BOUGHT A DOZEN NEW PINE BOARDS TO REPAIR YOUR FENCE AN' LEFT 'EM COVERED UP IN YOUR BACK YARD. YOU AN' YOUR FAMILY WENT TO FORT WORTH FOR THE WEEKEND, AN' WHEN YOU GOT BACK SUNDAY NIGHT THE LUMBER WAS GONE AN' BUCK'S SHED HAD SUDDENLY GOT A NEW ROOF.

YOU, BUCK, CLAIM ALL YOU DID WAS TO SAND AN' VARNISH THE OLD ROOF ON THE SATURDAY WALTER WAS GONE. THAT'S HOW COME IT LOOKS NEW AN' HAPPENS TO MATCH WALTER'S LUMBER. RIGHT?

YES SIR.

THAT'S ABOUT THE SIZE OF IT.

HE'S ALWAYS DOIN' THINGS LIKE THIS, SHERIFF. LONG AS I'VE LIVED HERE, BUCK ARLEN HAS TAKEN ADVANTAGE OF ME AN' POURED SCORN, I SAY SCORN, ON MY PROTESTS...

HELL, SHERIFF, LONG AS I'VE LIVED HERE OL' WALTER'S BEEN MAKIN' THESE DAMNFOOL PARANOID CLAIMS. I DON'T MIND THE BOY BEIN' CRAZY, BUT I SURE WOULD LIKE TO SEE HIM COME UP WITH SOME PROOF...

IT'S JUST LIKE HIGH NOON. I KNEW IT WOULD BE.

'KAY, HOW 'BOUT THIS:

BUCK, YOU AIN'T GOT NO OBJECTION, I'D LIKE TO TAKE A LOOK IN YOUR BACK YARD. I FIND ANY OL' ROTTED BOARDS LYIN' AROUND FROM, SAY, A RECENTLY REPLACED SHED ROOF, I KNOW YOU LIED TO ME. I DON'T, WELL...

HMMMM.

BE MY GUEST, SHERIFF, 'LONG AS YOU DON'T MIND WASTIN' HALF YOUR DAY. I GOT A LOTTA YARD BACK THERE.

HOW'D YOUR FENCE GET ALL SMASHED UP ANYHOW, WALTER?

THOSE DAMN QUINCANNON MEN, SHERIFF. START OF THE MONTH, SOME OF 'EM GOT DRUNK AN' KICKED MY FENCE DOWN IN A ACT OF WANTON, I SAY *WANTON*, VANDALISM...

AH, OL' WALTER'S RIGHT THERE, ACTUALLY. SAME BAD BOYS BURNED MY ROOF. CAME IN MY SHED TO SHIT ON MY LAWNMOWER AN' DROPPED A LIT CIGARETTE IN A CAN OF GASOLINE.

'COURSE, SINCE YOU STARTED, WE AIN'T HAD SO MUCH'VE THAT BULLSHIT...

YOU BOYS BOTH OWN BUSINESSES IN TOWN, DON'T YOU? QUINCANNON'S MEN QUIT COMIN' HERE, Y'ALL'RE GONNA LOSE A LOTTA INCOME.

YES SIR, THEY DO HAVE MONEY TO SPEND. BUT IT BARELY COVERS THE COST OF REPAIRING THE DAMAGE THEY CAUSE.

THAT'S A FACT.

uh-huh. WELL, LET'S SEE WHAT WE GOT HERE--

BE MY GUEST, SHERIFF, 'LONG AS YOU DON'T MIND STICKIN' YOUR HANDS IN A LOTTA SOILED TAMPONS AN' SANITARY TOWELS AN' ALL KINDSA AWFUL FEMALE MENSTRUAL BYPRODUCTS. MY OL' LADY JUST CAME OFF THE RAG.

... HELL, WHY NOT?

ALL YOURS, WALT.

AFTER ALL THIS TIME--

WELL, I SURE DO FEEL A WHOLE LOT BETTER FOR HAVIN' TOOK MY PUNISHMENT LIKE A MAN. YES SIR, THIS IS WHERE I BECOME A RESPONSIBLE CITIZEN ...

WORD OF ADVICE, WALTER?

DON'T DROP YOUR SHOULDER LIKE THAT 'FORE YOU SWING. HE'LL SEE WHAT'S COMIN', HAVE TIME TO GET READY.

HUH?

LIKE THAT.

BUCK WAKES UP, TELL HIM I'M HAVIN' A LITTLE MEETIN' TONIGHT TO TALK OVER THE QUINCANNON THING. SEVEN-THIRTY AT JODIE'S BAR AN' GRILL.

SEE YOU THERE.

I CAN'T BELIEVE YOU'RE INVOLVING AN ORGANIZATION LIKE THAT. NOT ONLY IS IT HIGHLY DANGEROUS, ON A PURELY MORAL LEVEL IT MAKES ME FEEL DEEPLY UNCOMFORTABLE...

MORAL LEVEL MY ASS, ODIN QUINCANNON'S BEEN A FULLY PAID-UP MEMBER SINCE NINETEEN FORTY-ONE. THEM FELLAS ARE HEROES AN' PATRIOTS AN' THAT'S ALL THERE IS TO IT.

ANYHOW, WHAT THE HELL'S GOT UP YOUR ASS? THOUGHT YOU'DA BEEN RIGHT BEHIND US, WITH ALL YOUR BIG HERO ADOLF HAD TO SAY 'BOUT NIGGERS AN' SUCH...

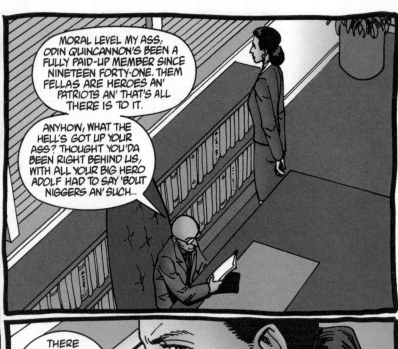

THERE IS *NO DIRECT EVIDENCE* THAT THE FÜHRER HELD RACIST VIEWS.

THERE AIN'T?

A VILE SMEAR ON THE PART OF HIS DETRACTORS. THAT ASPECT OF THE THIRD REICH HAS BEEN BLOWN OUT OF ALL PROPORTION.

BUT THEY GOT HIS SPEECHES ON TAPE! I FUCKIN' HEARD 'EM!

SPEECHES CAN BE *DUBBED*.

RIGHT, AN' I GUESS *MEIN KAMPF* WAS FORGED AN' HE GASSED ALL THEM KIKES FOR PUTTIN' UP THE INTEREST ON HIS CAR LOAN...

AS A MATTER OF FACT--

WE'RE GETTIN' OFF THE POINT, MISS OATLASH. NOW, THESE BOYS SAY THEY'RE GONNA TAKE A LOOK AT CUSTER--MAYBE TEST HIM A LITTLE BIT, SEE WHICH WAY HE JUMPS. I SAID I'D GO ALONG.

I GOT A FEELIN' IT'S GONNA BE WORTH IT...

I STOP QUINCANNON'S MEN FROM COMIN' INTO TOWN MUCH LONGER AN' THE SON OF A BITCH IS GONNA CUT UP ROUGH. AN' WHEN HE DOES THAT, I CAN'T AFFORD NO CRYIN' OR BACKIN' DOWN.

YOU FOLKS LIVE HERE. IT'S THE HOMES AN' BUSINESSES YOU OWN THAT MAKE SALVATION A COMMUNITY. I NEED TO BE CERTAIN 'FORE I TAKE ONE MORE STEP THAT THIS IS WHAT YOU WANT FROM ME, OR ELSE Y'ALL MAY AS WELL ELECT ANOTHER YES-MAN.

CLOSED

'KAY, SPEECH OVER. ANY QUESTIONS?

CORA?

HOW COME YOU INVITED THEM PEOPLE OVER THERE?

GREAT WHITE WHALE'S SORTA GOT HERSELF A POINT. WHEN THE LAW 'ROUND HERE EVER GIVE A DAMN 'BOUT FOLKS IN JOHN'S HOLLOW, ANYHOW?

YOU RECALL JIM BEWLEY ARRESTIN' A QUINCANNON MAN FOR TRESPASSIN' ON YOUR PROPERTY, MARVIN? 'CAUSE LAST WEEK ME AN' JESSE DID IT TWICE.

"JESSE", HUH?

er--

MAY I SAY SOME- THING?

THANK YOU.

PERHAPS MY VIEWS WILL LACK LEGITIMACY FOR SOME OF YOU. I WAS NOT BORN OR RAISED HERE. BUT IT SEEMS TO ME A VITAL POINT IS BEING OVER- LOOKED.

JUST BECAUSE SALVATION IS A TINY TOWN DOES NOT MEAN ITS PROBLEMS CAN BE IGNORED AS INSURMOUNT- ABLE. TO QUIT IN THE FACE OF DAUNTING ODDS--TO DISIN- TEGRATE IN OUR OWN APATHY AND PETTY DIFFERENCES BECAUSE WE CAN NO LONGER EVEN HOPE FOR VICTORY-- WOULD BE A TERRIBLE MISTAKE.

AND, IF I MAY BE SO BOLD, COMPLETELY CONTRARY TO THE SPIRIT OF THE LAND IN WHICH WE LIVE.

WHAT'S HE SAYIN'?

HE'S SAYIN' Y'ALL ARE TEXANS.

AN' IT'S UP TO YOU TO DECIDE WHAT THAT'S GONNA MEAN HERE.

IS IT A BUNCHA FAT, BIGOTED REDNECKS GIVIN' IN TO CROOKS AN' CORPORATIONS, 'CAUSE THEY'RE TOO BIG TO FIGHT AN' WE KINDA LIKE 'EM IN CHARGE OF US ANYHOW? WAY THE YANKEES SEE US?

CLOSED

OR IS IT DRAWIN' A LINE IN THE DUST AN' SAYIN' NO FURTHER.

I'LL FIGHT THE SON OF A BITCH.

YOU JUST SAY YES OR NO.

THANKS FOR SPEAKIN' UP LIKE YOU DID.

IT WAS MY PLEASURE.

THE PEOPLE HERE HAVE BEEN DESERTED. THEY HAVE SEEN LOCAL GOVERNMENT, AND UP 'TIL NOW THE LAW, BOUGHT AND TAKEN FROM THEM. TO WHOM DO THEY PROTEST? TO WHOM DO THEY GO FOR PROTECTION?

BUT YOU SPOKE OF *COMMUNITY*. AND THAT IS THE KEY. A COMMON PURPOSE FORGED WITHIN, NOT SOUGHT WITHOUT.

ALL I DID WAS REMIND THEM OF THAT.

THERE IS A CERTAIN VIEW THAT AMERICANS ARE LAZY, SELFISH PEOPLE. THAT THEY TAKE THE EASY OPTION, AND IF THAT OPTION IS TO KNUCKLE UNDER, SO BE IT.

BUT I DO NOT CHOOSE TO SUBSCRIBE TO THAT VIEW.

NOT THAT I AM IMBUING THE GOOD FOLK OF SALVATION WITH THE SPIRIT OF THE FRONTIER, OR ANYTHING SO GRAND. ALL THEY HAD TO DO WAS SEND THEIR HERO OUT TO FIGHT ON THEIR BEHALF.

SHERIFF'S JOB, AIN'T IT?

'SIDES.

I AIN'T NO HERO, GUNTHER.

TRIED IT ONCE. BUT IT DIDN'T TAKE.

LOOK!

IT'S THAT DAMN NIGGER GAL, JUST LIKE I TOLD YOU! HE'S PROBABLY PUTTIN' IT TO HER! THERE'S YOUR GODDAMN MISCEGENATION RIGHT THERE!

CALM DOWN, ODIN. LET'S SEE WHAT HAPPENS.

OFF YOU GO, BOYS...

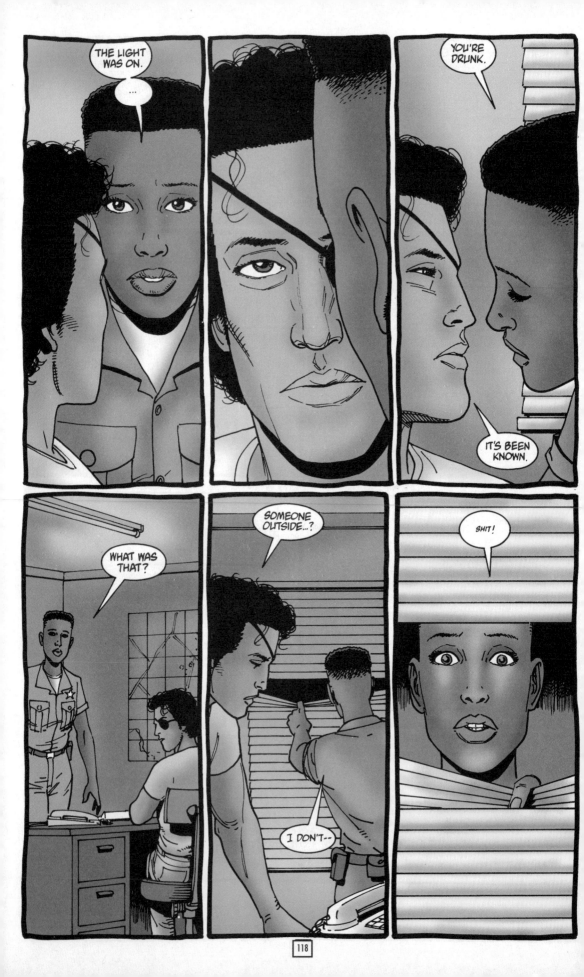

ASSHOLES...

THAT'S HIM! WATCH HIM NOW! WATCH HIM!

...

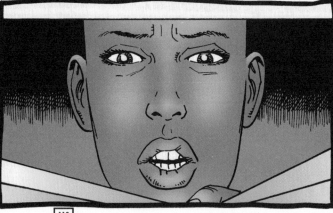

THINK WE GOT KLAN TROUBLE.

THINK SO?

OKAY, ODIN.

ABOUT LAST NIGHT...

KRAK

UH, YEAH. WELL I JUST APOLOGIZE LIKE HELL, CINDY. I AIN'T NEVER DONE NOTHIN' AS, UH, AS CRUDE AS THAT IN FRONT OF A LADY BEFORE.

I AIN'T GONNA GET SO DAMN DRUNK AGAIN, I PROMISE.

ACTUALLY... I MEANT BEFORE THAT. IN THE OFFICE.

OH.

WUFF-WUFF-WUFF.

WHITE MISCHIEF

GARTH ENNIS - Writer   **STEVE DILLON - Artist**

PAMELA RAMBO - Colorist   CLEM ROBINS - Letterer   AXEL ALONSO - Editor

PREACHER created by GARTH ENNIS and STEVE DILLON

PROBE THE ROOT...

UH, SORRY, MA'AM. MR. QUINCANNON AIN'T TO BE DISTURBED.

MA'AM, NO! HE SAID NO ONE AT ANY TIME! NOT IN HERE!

I'M HIS *LAWYER,* YOU IMBECILES. I CAN SEE HIM WHENEVER I WANT.

MA'AM, HE SAID ON PAIN OF *DEATH*--

OH, GET OUT OF THE WAY!

MR. QUIN-CANNON?

PROBE THE ROOT...

SIR...?

NIBBLE THE VEINS...

NIBBLE THE VEINS...

AND--

SAY THE NAME...

SAY THE NAME...

SAY THE NAME

AN' HAVE THE DAMN CAR CLEANED, TOO.

HELL'S WRONG WITH YOU, MISS OATLASH? YOU PREGNANT?

MUST'VE BEEN--SOMETHING I--ATE--

YEAH, PROBABLY PREGNANT. GODDAMN SPLIT-TAILS.

126

MR. QUINCANNON, REALLY, IF YOU INVOLVE THE *KLAN* IN THE MURDER OF A TOWN SHERIFF--HOW-EVER DUBIOUS HIS POSITION--THERE'S NOTHING I CAN DO TO PROTECT YOU. I'M ASKING YOU FOR THE LAST TIME TO GIVE IT UP...

LIKE HELL!

IN THAT CASE YOU LEAVE ME NO CHOICE. I'M OFFICIALLY TENDERING MY RESIGNATION AS YOUR--

YEAH, SURE! THAT'LL BE THE DAY!

WHERE THE HELL YOU GONNA FIND ANOTHER OPPORTUNITY LIKE THIS, MISS OATLASH?

WHERE YOU GONNA FIND SOMEONE'LL HIRE A WOMAN TO PRACTICE CORPORATE LAW AT A LEVEL THIS HIGH? SOME-ONE WITH THE KINDA MONEY CAN BUY A SENATOR? SOMEONE WILLIN' TO INDULGE YOUR GODDAMN HEATHEN NAZI PERVERSIONS, WITH A WORKFORCE DUMB ENOUGH TO VOLUNTEER FOR 'EM?

WHERE YOU GONNA FIND ANOTHER BOSS *LIKE ODIN...?*

CUSTER DIES TONIGHT, SO YOU BETTER JUST GET USED TO IT! YOU BE READY WITH THAT GODDAMN LEGAL MAGIC OF YOURS IN CASE THERE'S ANY SLIP-UPS, AN' LEAVE THE REST TO ME!

IT'S A TRAP.

BONE TREE
MIDNIGHT
A FRIEND

YEAH?

C'MON, REALLY, WHO'S GONNA WARN *US?* WE AIN'T GOT NO FRIENDS WOULD KNOW ABOUT THIS...

MAYBE NOT.

'CEPT I CAN THINK OF A DOZEN WAYS TO DRAW US IN BETTER'N THIS. WE'RE THE SHERIFF'S DEPARTMENT; ALL IT TAKES IS A CALL TO REPORT A INTRUDER OR SOMETHIN' AN' WE GO WHEREVER THEY WANT US.

...WHAT THE HELL'S A *BONE TREE?*

IT'S ON SAWYER ROAD ON THE WAY OUTTA TOWN. OL' BLASTED, DRIED-UP OAK STANDS APART FROM THE PINES.

I THINK I SEEN IT THE DAY I ARRIVED...

IT DIDN'T ALWAYS LOOK LIKE THAT. BACK IN THE FIFTIES IT WAS FIVE TIMES AS HIGH, HAD GREAT LONG BRANCHES AN' GREEN LEAVES ALL OVER IT.

HAD LYNCH ROPES HANGIN' FROM IT, TOO.

BUT ONE NIGHT IN FIFTY-NINE THE KLAN STRUNG UP SOME BOYS FROM THE HOLLOW, THREE BROTHERS BY THE NAME OF BRYSON, AN' THE STORY GOES THAT LIGHTNIN' STRUCK THE TREE AN' BURNED IT DOWN WITH THE BRYSONS STILL KICKIN' ON THEIR ROPES.

"AS PROOF GOD HATED NIGGERS."

AFTER THAT IT SORTA ENTERED KLAN MYTHOLOGY.

WHAT I KNOW OF THE LORD, I GUESS IT WOULDN'T SURPRISE ME.

IT'S SHITTY, CINDY.

IT'S THE SOUTH.

HAVE YOU SEEN THOSE TWO?

MM?

GUNSLINGERS, SHARING ONE LAST DRINK BEFORE DOING WHAT THEY'VE GOT TO DO. THAT'S WHAT THEY REMIND ME OF.

I WONDER WHAT THEY'RE UP TO...

ME TOO.

YOU THINK THERE'S SOMETHING BETWEEN THEM, GUNTHER?

I WOULD BE VERY SURPRISED IF THERE WAS NOT. BUT I IMAGINE JESSE IS CURRENTLY PREOCCUPIED WITH HIS FIRST LOVE.

WHICH IS?

HIS DUTY. I'VE KNOWN MEN LIKE HIM BEFORE.

MOSTLY SOLDIERS.

AND MOSTLY DEAD?

SOME OF THEM. OTHERS GROW OLD, FATHER A BROOD OF YOUNG, SPEND THEIR TIME WONDERING WHY THEY MADE IT HOME AND NOT THE BOYS WHO DIED BESIDE THEM.

THEY WONDER WHAT DIFFERENCE THEIR DUTY HAS MADE, BUT NEVER ONCE BETRAY IT.

THEIR MOTHERS ARE ALWAYS BEAUTIFUL, OF COURSE.

THOSE TWO'RE GETTIN' KINDA COZY, AIN'T THEY?

SO THEY ARE.

THAT BOTHER YOU?

I AIN'T SURE.

GUNTHER'S A REAL NICE GUY...

GUNTHER'S A SWELL GUY. BUT IT'S MY *MOM*, YOU KNOW?

DAMN, WHAT IS IT ABOUT TOUGH GUYS AN' THEIR MOTHERS? *SHE'S* THE ONE S'POSED TO WORRY ABOUT YOU.

HEY, IF SHE WAS MRS. HAHN, I GUESS THAT'D SORTA MAKE HIM YOUR DADDY, WOULDN'T IT?

NO IT WOULDN'T.

THERE'S MY LITTLE *HECTOR...!* I WON'T LET THE NASTY MEN TELL NO MORE MEXICAN JOKES!

'LESS THEY'RE FUNNY ONES, THAT IS! *HAAAAWW!*

ELEVEN-TWENTY. TIME TO VENTURE FORTH AN' DO BATTLE ON BEHALF OF THE GOOD FOLK OF SALVATION...

THEY MAY BE REDNECKS, BUT THEY'RE *OUR* REDNECKS.

YOU GOT THE PLAN STRAIGHT?

AYE-FIRMATIVE.

FIVE DOWN IS *ALAMO,* TOBY.

"REMEMBERED IN TEXAS"? REALLY?

YOU TWO LEAVING ALREADY?

YES MA'AM.

WELL...BE CAREFUL, WILL YOU? WHAT ARE YOU DOING OUT THIS LATE, ANYWAY?

WHAT WE GOTTA.

NIGHT, MOM.

...GUT THE SON OF A BITCH LIKE A GOD-DAMN CATFISH AN' MAKE THAT COON BITCH OF HIS LAP UP THE MESS...

NOW ODIN TELLS US THIS FELLA AIN'T EVEN BEEN PROPERLY APPOINTED --SO WE DO HIM AN' THE FEDS OR THE RANGERS LOOK INTO IT, THEY GONNA FIND SO MUCH SHIT WE GONNA BE LONG GONE BY THE TIME THEY FINISH.

'KAY, ANY QUESTIONS?

I GOT ONE.

YOU LADIES MAKE THEM DRESSES YOUR-SELVES OR YOU BUY 'EM FROM CRACKERS-R-US?

IT'S HIM!

MISTER--

YOU ARE FUCKIN' DEAD.

FIRST OFF, I THINK WE'LL HAVE THEM DUMB-LOOKIN' MASKS OFF...

FUCK YOU--

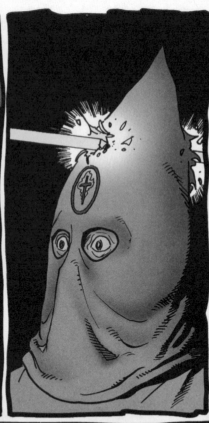

HOODS OFF, BOYS! NOW!

JESUS CHRIST.

WHY IS IT THE GREATEST CHAMPIONS OF THE WHITE RACE ALWAYS TURN OUT TO BE THE WORST EXAMPLES OF IT? YOU!

WH-WH-WH--?

WHERE THE FUCK IS YOUR CHIN?

I SWEAR.

ANYHOW...I COULD HAVE YOU TRASH SHOT DOWN HERE AN' NOW, SAVE US ALL A LOTTA TROUBLE. OR HELL, YOU KNOW WHAT I COULD DO? I COULD *TELL YOU* TO GET THE HELL OUTTA HERE AN' GO BE BETTER PEOPLE, AN' *YOU WOULD...*

YEAH, *RIGHT--!*

SHIT YOUR- SELF.

BUT I AIN'T GONNA DO EITHER'VE THEM THINGS, 'CAUSE THAT AIN'T WHERE MY AUTHORITY COMES FROM IN THIS INSTANCE.

SO WHERE DOES IT COME FROM, EXACTLY?

WHY, FROM MY BEIN' A LAW OFFICER OF THE GREAT STATE OF TEXAS. WHICH MEANS I CAN KICK YOUR REDNECK ASSES HALF TO DEATH AN' ALL YOU CAN DO IS ASK FOR MORE.

SO YOU CAN KICK OUR ASSES, HUH?

ONE AT A TIME OR ALL TOGETHER, TURD-BREATH.

GARY?

KICK GARY'S ASS, SHERIFF. THEN TALK SOME MORE SHIT, YOUR MOUTH'S STILL WHERE IT USED TO BE.

YOU MADE A *BIG MISTAKE,* FELLA.

THAT A FACT?

GODDAMN RIGHT, FUCKIN' WITH ME.

USED TO BE JUST LIKE YOU, SEE. LITTLE GUY. SURE, I WAS TALL, BUT I DIDN'T HAVE NO MUSCLE MASS. GOT PICKED ON ALL THE TIME BY THEM BIG SPEAR-CHUCKERS LIKED TO PLAY BASKETBALL.

THEN I SAW A ADVERT IN *BEEFCAKE MAGAZINE,* SHOWIN' THIS BOOK 'BOUT BUILDIN' MUSCLE MASS. WROTE OFF AN' GOT THE FREE STEROID COURSE CAME WITH THE HARDBACK EDITION. LEARNED SOME KINDA CHINK ZEN THING 'BOUT FOCUSIN' YORE WILL ON YORE BODY WHEN YOU WORK OUT.

BUILT MYSELF THIGHS OF IRON.

ARMS OF STEEL.

PECS OF *ROCK.*

BALLS OF MUSH.

WAAAAAHH!!

I COULD KILL A THOUSAND OF YOU ASSHOLES, OR ORDER YOU TO GO TO HELL, AN' A THOUSAND MORE'D GROW FROM THE SAME OL' SHIT. SO I'M GONNA DO LIKE YOU DO: I'M GONNA MAKE *FEAR* MY WEAPON. EVERYBODY READY?

NOW FEAR THIS:

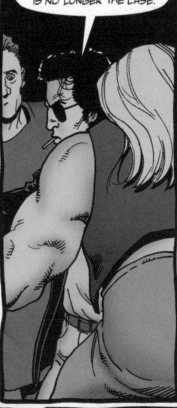

I KNOW YOU SCUM REGARD THIS PLACE AS PARTA THE HISTORY OF YOUR FUCKED-UP LITTLE CRACKER CONVENTION. BE ADVISED THAT SO LONG AS IT FALLS WITHIN THE ENVIRONS OF SALVATION, THAT IS NO LONGER THE CASE.

THIS TOWN IS OFF-LIMITS TO SHEET-WEARIN' MOTHERFUCKERS LIKE YOU. I HAD MY WAY, EVERY HATEMONGERIN' PIECE OF SHIT ON THE PLANET THINKS HE'S GOD'S CHOSEN JUST BECAUSE'VE HIS COLOR WOULD BE STRONGLY ENCOURAGED TO GET THE FUCK OFF OF IT. MAN JUDGES ANOTHER BY HIS SKIN AIN'T WORTHY TO BE CALLED ONE.

NOW YOU GATHER UP YOUR GARBAGE--INCLUDIN' BRAINS OF SHIT HERE--AN' YOU GO ON HOME TO YOUR FAT OL' KLAN SOWS. AN' THE NEXT TIME YOU'RE PLANNIN' SOMETHIN' STUPID YOU PRAY TO FUCKIN' JESUS SOMEONE LIKE ME DON'T TAKE A INTEREST. WE *ARE* OUT THERE.

MESSAGE ENDS.

HEY, FUCK YOU, CUSTER! YOU DON'T TELL US HOW TO LIVE, NOT 'TIL YOU SEEN YOUR WAY OF LIFE GETTIN' SWALLOWED UP BY GODDAMN ALIEN CULTURES!

HUH?

OH YEAH, I HEARD THAT'N BEFORE. "YOU AIN'T BEEN WHERE WE HAVE, SO HOW CAN YOU GIVE US SHIT FOR ACTIN' LIKE SAVAGES?" FUCK YOU...

YOU COME ALONG WITH ME, BOSS MAN. WE STILL GOT SOME MATTERS TO DISCUSS.

AAAAAOOOW...!

WELL FUCK HIM, HUH, FELLAS? WE AIN'T LETTIN' HIM GET AWAY WITH THAT, RIGHT?

LET'S KICK HIS NIGGER-LOVIN' ASS!

FELLAS?

FELLAS...!

FELLAAAAAAHHS!!

WH-WH-WHY IS SHE DRIVIN' SO FAST?

SHE LIKES IT. SO I GUESS YOU'RE THE GRAND SHITHEAD OF THAT LITTLE KLAVERN, HUH?

uh...GRAND CYCLOPS...

MORE NORMALLY KNOWN AS *JAMES EDGAR BEAUREGARD*, OWNER OF THE FUR CREEK STRIP CLUB AN' OTHER SUCH BUSINESSES IN AN' AROUND HOUSTON.

F.B.I.s GOT A FILE ON YOU A MILE LONG, JIMBO. INCLUDIN' THE SEAT-SNIFFIN' THING.

B-BUT I EXPLAINED ALL ABOUT THAT!

YOU PAID OFF THE TROOPER ARRESTED YOU, YOU MEAN.

JOHN'S HOLLOW

LISTEN UP, SHITBIRD: TO ME YOU AN' YOUR FOOLS AIN'T NOTHIN' BUT WORMS CRAWLIN' IN THE NIGHT. YOU AIN'T EVEN GOT THE BALLS TO SHOW YOUR DAMN FACES.

BUT YOU CAN'T HIDE FROM ME. YOU CAN'T BUY ME AN' YOU SURE AS HELL CAN'T KILL ME. EVERY WAY YOU LOOK AT IT, I GOT YOU BEAT.

I GOT YOU BUFFALOED.

NOW GET THE FUCK OUT!!

WHA-- NO--

AAAAAAHHH!!

AAAAH! AWHH! AAAHH!

LAWSY ME AN' OTHER SUCH UTTERANCES. A FELLA ATTIRED IN THE MANNER OF A WELL-KNOWN RACIST ORGANIZATION.

"PECKER-WOOD WALKS TO HOUSTON NAKED."

NOW SPORTS.

SO WHAT-- *HNNNHH--*

YOU GONNA DO-- *GUHHH--*

NOW, MR. QUINCANNON--?

THROW A BARBECUE.

I'M GONNA BURN THAT FUCKIN' TOWN CLEAR DOWN TO THE GROUND.

TO BE CONTINUED

YOU GOT A TWO-GALLON KEG OF NAPALM BEHIND EACH BUILDIN'. DETONATORS'RE STUCK ON WITH STRIPS OF C4.

THAT I LIKE THE SOUND OF...

TRANSMITTER. PRESS THE TOP BUTTON ONCE AN' THE FIRST CHARGE GOES UP, THE ONE AT THE SHERIFF'S OFFICE LIKE YOU SAID. EACH SUCCESSIVE PUSH OF THAT BUTTON WILL SET OFF ANOTHER ONE, UP TO A TOTAL OF TWENTY-THREE.

AN' YOU'RE IN A HURRY, THE SECOND BUTTON'LL DO 'EM ALL AT ONCE.

AN' YOU COVERED EVERY PLACE ON THE MAIN STREET? DIDN'T NOBODY SEE YOU?

TIME OF NIGHT I DID IT, LOCAL FUCKS'RE EITHER SNORIN' OR RUTTIN'. WEREN'T NO BIG THING.

SO YOU'RE SURE THIS IS ALL WIRED UP OKAY? 'CAUSE THE LAST BOY OL' ODIN BROUGHT IN, THE JOB HE DID WASN'T WORTH A HANDFULLA ASSFLAKES...

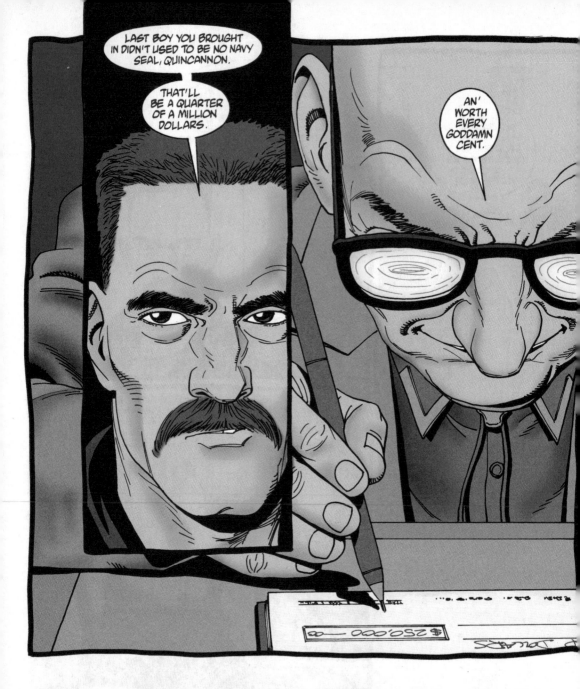

JESSE GET YOUR GUN

GARTH ENNIS - Writer   STEVE DILLON - Artist

PAMELA RAMBO - Colorist   **CLEM ROBINS** - Letterer   **AXEL ALONSO** - Editor

PREACHER created by **GARTH ENNIS** and **STEVE DILLON**

DAYS TURN INTO WEEKS AN' THE WEEKS TURN INTO MONTHS, HUH, SKEET?

WUFF...

THE MOST PEACEFUL MONTHS IN THE RECENT HISTORY OF SALVATION, IN FACT. I TRUST THE GOOD SHERIFF WILL ALLOW ME TO BUY HIM A BEER?

JUST THE ONE. I GOT ALL THIS WHISKEY TO DRINK 'FORE I START WORK.

HERE'S TO YOU, GUNTHER.

AND TO YOU. THE JOB IS AS DEMANDING AS EVER, THEN?

COULD BE. BUT HE AIN'T DONE YET, NOT BY A LONG WAY. I SEEN FELLAS LIKE HIM BEFORE; HE'S OUT AT THAT PLANTA HIS AN' US BEATIN' HIM AS BAD AS WE DID IS EATIN' AT HIS GUT LIKE A *CANCER.*

NO, ONLY ONE WAY THIS IS GONNA END.

THESE ARE ON THE HOUSE.

OH, MAN. WAY THIS IS GOIN', CRIME IN SALVATION'S GONNA RUN RAMPANT...

WAY *WHAT'S* GOING TO END?

NOTHIN', MOM.

I'LL BET. YOU BE CAREFUL, JESSE. I DON'T WANT YOU GOING AROUND THINKING YOU'RE THE LONE RANGER.

C'MON, I'M S'POSED TO BE THE SHERIFF 'ROUND HERE...

YES, AND I'M THE SHERIFF'S MOTHER AROUND HERE. YOU'LL DO AS YOU'RE TOLD.

GUNTHER, I HAVE YOUR REMINGTON DOCUMENTARY BEHIND THE BAR. THANKS FOR LOANING IT TO ME. IT WAS EXCELLENT.

JESUS...

MY PLEASURE. REMIND ME TO SHOW YOU MY SET OF HIS PRINTS ON THURSDAY NIGHT.

YES, WHAT ARE YOU COOKING FOR ME?

EVENIN', BOSS!

HEY, CINDY. ALL QUIET ON THE WESTERN FRONT?

YOU KNOW IT. WAY THINGS ARE AROUND HERE, TWO OF US'LL HAVE TO DO SOMETHIN' OURSELVES TO SPICE THINGS UP.

I'M GOIN' OVER TO KILKANE FOR CHINESE FOOD. YOU WANT SOME?

THAT'D BE REAL GOOD. 'LONG AS YOU DON'T START SHOWIN' OFF WITH THEM DAMN CHOPSTICKS AGAIN, 'KAY?

THEN IT'S A DATE. SEE YOU IN THE OFFICE IN A HOUR OR TWO.

WHAT?

GODDAMMIT...!

JUST GOOD FRIENDS, OKAY?

MORE FOOL YOU, THEN. SHE LIKES YOU MORE THAN FRIENDS, AND YOU KNOW IT.

DON'T YOU LIKE GIRLS?

HEH! GUNTHER, I GET DOWN ON MY KNEES EVERY MORNIN' AN' GIVE ETERNAL THANKS FOR THE EXISTENCE OF GIRLS IN A OTHERWISE POINTLESS UNIVERSE...

OF COURSE.

SO WHAT'S STOPPING YOU?

MONEY ALWAYS WINS, MISS OATLASH.

THAT'S WHAT BOYS LIKE THAT CUSTER FELLA NEVER DO GET. I OFFERED TO PAY HIM AN' PAY HIM WELL, BUT HE CHOSE TO FIGHT ME. TOOK ONE LOOK AT OL' ODIN AN' FIGURED HE COULD WIN, YES SIR.

BUT IT AIN'T WHAT YOU LOOK LIKE, OR HOW TOUGH YOU ARE, OR ANYTHIN' ELSE 'CEPT WHAT YOU CAN *AFFORD*...

AIN'T GOT WHAT IT TAKES TO WIN? NO BIGGIE. JUST GO ON OUT AN' BUY IT.

HELL, I RECALL ME AN' SOME FRIENDS SAVED UP AN' BOUGHT OURSELVES A PRESIDENT ONCE.

REALLY?

YEAH, 'CEPT THE DUMB BASTARD MADE A MESS OF IT. ROYALLY SCREWED THE POOCH.

WAY THIS COUNTRY WORKS, MISS OATLASH. MONEY GREASIN' THE WHEELS. DON'T LET NOBODY TELL YOU DIFFERENT.

YOU'D BETTER HOPE SO, MR. QUIN-CANNON. PRODUCTIVITY AT THE PLANT HAS DROPPED AWAY TO ALMOST NOTHING. ANOTHER DOZEN MEN LEFT THIS AFTERNOON.

THERE'S STILL A GUARD ON SHED NUMBER FOUR, AIN'T THERE? THE COLDSTORE?

BIG FUCKIN' DEAL, SO WE LOST A FEW MONTHS' TURNOVER, THEY'LL COME BACK WHEN CUSTER'S GONE, YOU JUST SEE IF THEY--

THE COLD-STORE... OH, YES. AS PER YOUR SPECIFIC INSTRUCTIONS.

GODDAMN RIGHT. AIN'T NOBODY GOES IN THERE 'CEPT ODIN.

ODIN... AN' HIS MEAT...

ALONE WITH HIS MEAT...

WHAT ARE YOU GOING TO DO WITH THE SHERIFF?

HUH? OH, I'M GONNA DESTROY SALVATION IN FRONT OF HIS EYES AN' THEN BRING HIM BACK HERE TO TORTURE HIS ASS TO DEATH.

OVER A COUPLE OF MONTHS, 'COURSE. JUST SO HE SEES THE BOYS COMIN' BACK, THE PLANT STARTIN' UP AGAIN, SOME OTHER STUPID LITTLE TOWN 'ROUND HERE ROLLIN' OVER AN' STICKIN' ITS ASS UP FOR ODIN LIKE A TWO-DOLLAR WHORE...

JUST SO HE KNOWS HE NEVER MADE NO DIFFERENCE AFTER ALL.

AND YOU EXPECT JE-- SHERIFF CUSTER TO SIT STILL FOR THIS?

MISS OATLASH, I 'SPECT THE SON OF A BITCH TO COME ALONG IN HERE MEEK AS A LAMB.

EVEN AS WE SPEAK, STEPS ARE BEIN' TAKEN TO ENSURE IT.

Y'ALL NEED ANY HELP?

DOH--

BUDD YUH DUH, BIDTH.

GUB YUH HUNDTH UHN THUD UN GUD UHDA THUH KUHH. THLUHLY.

WHAT?

HE, HE SAID KEEP YOUR HANDS IN SIGHT AND GET OUT OF THE--

NAD FUGGIG THYERIFF DUD THUZZA MUH!

HUH?

THUDDUB! HUNDTH UHNA UHNUH UHH! GUDD UHNUH TRUNG!

uh...MAYBE IF I DID THE TALKING...

YEAH, OR GOT THIS MOTHERFUCKER SOME SUBTITLES--

THUDDUB!

ME AN' CINDY GET ON REAL WELL. WE SIT UP 'TIL DAWN DRINKIN' AN' TALKIN'. I LIKE HER, SHE LIKES ME, SHE ALL BUT INVITED ME HOME A COUPLE TIMES BUT SHE'S WAITIN' FOR ME TO MAKE A MOVE--

SHIT...

MUST BE EMPTY.

BUT WHAT'S STOPPING ME? YOU GOT ME THERE.

DAMMIT, PILGRIM...

A FELLA COULD GO CRAZY WAITIN' FOR YA TA LIGHT THAT THING. HERE!

AN' YA KNOW WHAT'S STOPPIN' YA. IT AIN'T GOT NOTHIN' TA DO WITH HER.

IT'S THE OTHER LITTLE GAL, AIN'T IT?

HELL, PILGRIM. YA KNOW ANY OTHER KIND **WORTH A DAMN?**

NO. NO I DON'T.

SEE...BEFORE THE VALLEY, THE BOMB AN' ALL, I KNEW IT'D GET BAD. I JUST NEVER IMAGINED HOW BAD.

THAT'S WHY I DON'T FEEL RIGHT 'BOUT GOIN' BACK TO ALLA THAT. 'CAUSE THEY'RE A PARTA IT. CASSIDY...AN'...

THAT RIGHT THERE IS WHAT'S STICKIN' IN MY CRAW. THE THOUGHTA THEM TOGETHER LIKE THAT, NOT A MONTH AFTER WHAT HAPPENED.

OH SHIT, THE THOUGHTA HER WITH *ANYONE ELSE AT ALL*-- AFTER EVERYTHING WE DID AN' SAID AN' SWORE, THAT JUST 'BOUT CUTS THE GODDAMN HEART OUTTA ME.

'CAUSE TULIP'S...

IF I'M TO FINISH THIS THING I GOTTA BE AT MY BEST. AN' WITHOUT HER I'M NO MORE'N A DAMN SHADOW.

WITHOUT THAT GIRL I'M NOTHIN'.

THEN I GUESS YA KNOW WHAT YA GOTTA DO, DON'T YA?

I GUESS SO.

158

WUFF! WARRF! WARRFFF!

YEAH, I KNOW. STORM'S COMIN' IN.

CINDY, WHERE ARE YOU, GIRL? ME AN' YOU GOTTA HAVE OURSELVES A TALK...

FOR YOU.

CINDY?

NO...IT ACTUALLY SOUNDS LIKE--

DAMN!!

★ SHERIFF ★

Heh, heh, heh, heh, heh...

QUINCANNON?!

YOU LITTLE FUCKIN' COCKSUCKER, WHAT THE HELL ARE YOU DOIN'?

WHY, I'M THROWIN' A PARTY, SHERIFF. AN' YOU DON'T WANT THE RESTA SALVATION NAPALMED AN' YORE NIGGER WHORE FUCKED AN' BUTCHERED, YOU BETTER GET YORE ASS ALONG TO IT.

HERE'S WHAT YOU DO:

159

UH--YESSIR, WE GOT HER... SHE JUST CAN'T COME TO THE PHONE RIGHT NOW, IS ALL...

AN' WHY NOT, GODDAMMIT?

WELL WE--UH--WE HIT HER KINDA HARD WHEN WE GOT HER, SEE, AN' SHE AIN'T QUITE WOKE UP YET...

WELL, SOON'S SHE DOES YOU CALL ME--

BA-DAM
FUCK!

WHAT THE HELL WAS THAT?

THAT-- THAT WAS THUNDER, SIR--

I AIN'T SO SURE YOU GOT SHIT, QUINCANNON.

OH YEAH?

I GOT THIS, MOTHERFUCKER! MATTER OF FACT, YOU TAKE A REAL GOOD LOOK AT YOUR PRECIOUS LITTLE TOWN DOWN THERE! 'CAUSE I TELL YOU, IT'S GONNA BE YORE LAST!

SON OF A BITCH--

KEEP YORE DISTANCE! REMEMBER THE NIGGER!

NO, SALVATION'S GONNA BURN, IT'S GONNA FRY LIKE FUCKIN' BACON IN FRONTA YORE EYES AN' AIN'T NOTHIN' YOU CAN DO TO STOP IT! AN' THEN YOU, ME AN' THE JUNGLE BUNNY'RE GONNA HAVE OURSELVES A PARTY YOU'LL NEVER FORGET!

SO HERE IT COMES! WATCH AN' LEARN, YOU FUCK! HERE'S EVERYTHIN' YOU FOUGHT TO PROTECT GONE IN A FUCKIN' INSTANT!

HERE IT COMES!!

WHAT...
THE
HELL...?

WELL,
THAT WAS
PRETTY FUCKIN'
LUCKY...!

NUHHHHHH

JESUS!!

OH HECTOR, I'M SORRY I CALLED YOU A DUMB BEANER...

WE GOTTA GET HIM OVER THERE *NOW*--

HUH? SHIT!

HEY, WHERE'S THE EVIL DUDE?

ASSHOLE MIGHT STILL HAVE CINDY. I'M GONNA HAVE TO GO GET HIM.

ALONE?

YEAH, *ALONE!*

I TOLD YOU FOLKS TO STAY OUTTA THIS AN' I MEANT IT, GODDAMMIT! NOW Y'ALL GET THIS BOY OUTTA HERE AN' LEAVE THAT PIGFUCKER TO ME, AN' BY GOD I WILL FINISH THIS ONCE AN' FOR ALL!

WUFF!

JESUS! 'KAY, YOU COME IF YOU FUCKIN' WANT...

WUFF!

MM.

FAR AS YOU GO, BUDDY. THIS ASSHOLE'S GONE CRAZIER'N A LIZARD WITH A SUNSTROKE AN' I DON'T WANT YOU STOPPIN' A BULLET...

GUHH--!

UHN

NOW, MY DARLING.
MY *SUPERMAN.*

YOU ARE MY
ARYAN DREAM,
JESSE CUSTER. MY
ULTIMATE PHYSICAL
IDEAL. OUR JOINING
WILL BE A TRIUMPH
OF *NATIONAL
SOCIALIST
PURITY.*

YOU ARE
ALMOST PERFECT,
DARLING...

ALMOST.

TO BE
CONTINUED

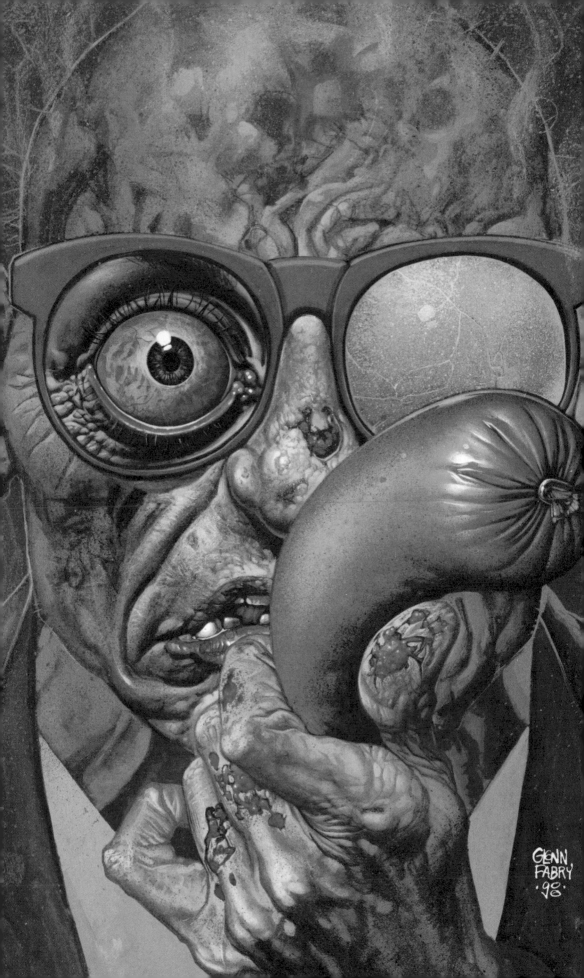

SINCE THE MOMENT I SAW YOU I HAVE *WANTED* YOU...

THIS WILL BE THE LOVE OF *GODS*, DARLING. OF *VALKYRIE* AND *NIBELUNG*.

YOUR ENTRY WILL BE LIKE *LIGHTNING*. YOU WILL *INVADE ME, OCCUPY ME*--AND JUST WHEN I CAN TAKE NO MORE YOU WILL OPEN UP A *SECOND FRONT*...

THIS WILL BE...

BLITZKRIEG...

IN YOUR *NAME!*

RRRAARRGGH, *FUCK ME!*

FUCK ME HARD AND CALL ME EVA!

AAH--! CHRIST, YOU SCARED ME! HOW DID YOU GET IN?

AIN'T NO ONE LOCKS THEIR DOORS 'ROUND HERE, GUNTHER. YOU OUGHTTA KNOW THAT, BEIN' SUCH A CHAMPION OF SMALL-TOWN TEXAS.

JESSE, IT IS NEARLY FOUR A.M.... WHAT IS THIS ABOUT?

'BOUT A BOOK I FOUND IN MISS OATLASH'S PLACE THIS MORNIN', 'FORE I SENT HER THINGS ON TO THE BIN. GAL'S GOT SHIT YOU WOULDN'T BELIEVE.

JAGERS: FIGHTER ACES OF THE LUFTWAFFE

BUT--

SO I SAW THIS AN' I THOUGHT HEY, MAYBE THEY GOT SOMETHIN' IN HERE 'BOUT GUNTHER'S BROTHER, AN' THEY DO.

AN' RIGHT AFTER IT THEY GOT "MAJOR HAHN'S YOUNGER BROTHER GUNTHER ALSO JOINED J.G. FIFTY-THREE, BUT WAS SHOT DOWN AND KILLED BY HURRICANES OF FIVE-OH-ONE SQUADRON ON OCTOBER EIGHTEENTH, WITHOUT HAVING OPENED HIS SCORE."

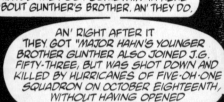

"HIS BODY WAS WASHED ASHORE AT WISSANT THREE DAYS LATER."

WHO THE HELL ARE YOU?

I-- LOOK-- WAIT--

I CALLED THE IMMIGRATION PEOPLE. THEY GOT YOU COMIN' INTO SAN DIEGO-- UNDER THE VAN DER POL NAME--IN JUNE *FORTY-SIX*, WHICH IS THREE YEARS LATER'N YOU SAID BEFORE.

THE TRUTH.

PLEASE, GIVE ME A CHANCE--

THE *TRUTH*.

MY NAME IS SIEGFRIED VECHTEL--!

HOW DID YOU... HOW...

I FOUND HAHN'S NAME IN THE RECORDS... HE WASN'T EVEN A *FOOTNOTE* IN HISTORY, I NEVER THOUGHT I'D BE CAUGHT OUT...

WHY NOT JUST INVENT A NAME?

I NEEDED... I WANTED THERE TO BE A KIND OF TRUTH TO IT. FOR ME AS MUCH AS ANY- BODY ELSE.

Uh-huh. PILOT LOSES HIS BROTHER, SHARP KINDA FELLA, FOOLS HIS BOSSES INTO SENDIN' HIM TO SPY IN AMERICA. REAL ROGUE.

NICE *SAFE* SORTA EX-NAZI.

DO YOU KNOW WHAT A POLICE BATTALION WAS?

...I THINK I DO.

THEY THE BOYS WENT IN AFTER THE FIGHTIN' WAS OVER? WEHRMACHT OCCUPIED TERRITORY, THEN THE POLICE BATTALIONS CAME AN' TURNED FOLKS INTO SLAVES?

OR JUST PLAIN FUCKIN' *KILLED* 'EM?

WHOLE VILLAGES. REGIONS. ACROSS POLAND, THE BALKANS, THE CRIMEA...

ON AND ON IT WENT, NEVERENDING. DIG A PIT OUTSIDE OF TOWN, LINE THEM UP, A COUPLE OF MACHINE-GUNNERS...

AND LATER, CHRIST, LATER-- IN THE CAMPS--

I HAD TO, THEY GAVE ME ORDERS AND I *HAD TO*... YOU DON'T UNDERSTAND WHAT IT WAS *LIKE*, THEN...

SHIT, DON'T EVEN FUCKIN' *TRY* THAT'N.

HMH.

SAID ALL THE RIGHT GODDAMN THINGS, DIDN'T YOU?

WHAT...?

YOU SEE THIS NEW FELLA IN TOWN, THIS REDNECK SHERIFF STIRRIN' SHIT UP, YOU THINK HEY, WHY DON'T I FUCK WITH THIS ASSHOLE A LITTLE BIT...

YOU TELL YOUR DAMN STORY AN' IT SOUNDS REAL GOOD; IT'S KINDA FUNNY AN' CHARMIN' AN' IT'S EVEN PARTLY TRUE, 'CEPT IT HAPPENED TO SOMEBODY ELSE. THAT SURE THROWS HIM OFF THE SCENT.

AN' THEN, HELL, YOU REALLY GO TO TOWN. ALL THAT MEN OF HONOR STUFF, ALL THAT DOWN-HOME BULLSHIT. *THE MYTH OF AMERICA*, WASN'T THAT WHAT YOU SAID?

GOTTA HAND IT TO YOU, GUNTHER. ONE LOOK AT ME AN' YOU KNEW JUST WHICH BUTTONS TO PUSH.

THAT-- OH MY GOD-- THAT WASN'T IT *AT ALL*...!

IT WAS *TRUE*, JESSE! ALL OF IT, I MEANT EVERY WORD OF IT!

I *DO* LOVE THIS COUNTRY! I ALWAYS HAVE, WITH ALL MY HEART! DON'T YOU SEE AMERICA IS MY *SECOND CHANCE*...?

I HAVE DONE TERRIBLE THINGS. I HAVE COMMITTED *NIGHTMARES* AGAINST HUMANITY. BUT I ESCAPED FROM THAT TIME AND CAME HERE, AND I LOVED THIS PLACE BECAUSE IN IT I SAW HOW I COULD REDEEM MY SINS: HOW I COULD CAST THE OLD WORLD ASIDE AND REJOICE IN THE NEW ONE, WHICH IS THE GOD-GIVEN RIGHT OF ALL AMERICANS.

I HAVE LIVED A GOOD LIFE IN THE TIME THAT I'VE HAD HERE. I BELIEVED THAT IF I DID, AMERICA WOULD REACH OUT AND POINT THE WAY TO MY REDEMPTION.

AND AFTER ALL THIS TIME, YOU CAME.

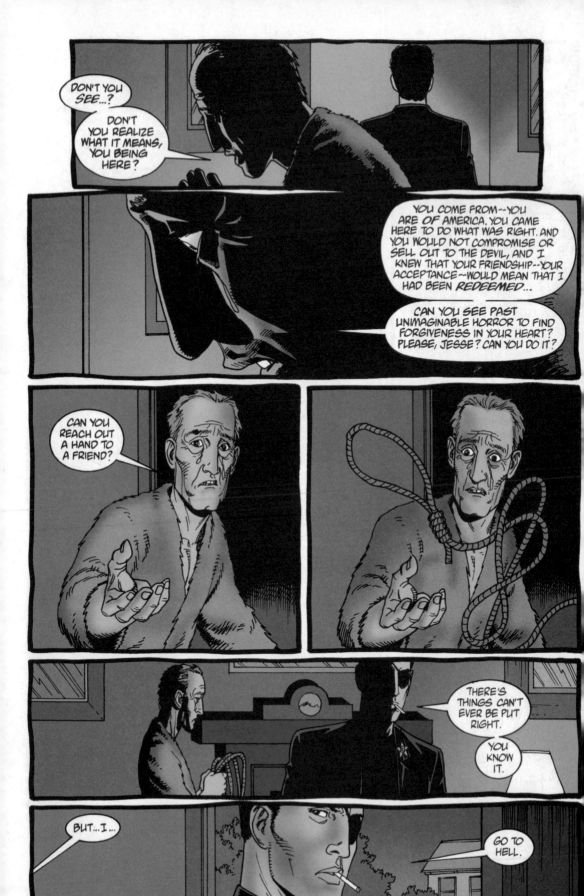

I'M REAL SORRY YOUR BROTHEL BURNED DOWN, JESSE.

DON'T YOU WORRY NONE, LORIE. IT WASN'T MUCH OF A, *uh*, A BROTHEL TO BEGIN WITH.

YOU'RE GOING TO LEAVE US SOON, AREN'T YOU? I SAW A BAG PACKED ON THE FRONT SEAT OF YOUR ELEPHANT.

YEAH, ALL MY WORLDLY GOODS...SHIT, LOOK AT THIS. LITTLE BASTARD DIDN'T EVEN LEAVE ME A POT TO PISS IN.

I'LL MISS YOU. I THINK A LOT OF PEOPLE WILL.

WELL HELL, I'LL MISS YOU TOO, LORIE ...uh...

FIVE ACROSS-- "JOHN WAYNE," DEE SOMETHIN', KAY SOMETHIN'...DAMN, WHAT COULD THAT BE?

JODIE'S BA

TOBY?

YEAH, DUDE?

...NOTHIN'.

SURE, DUDE.

SO.

YOU'RE LEAVING TONIGHT, THEN? HAVEN'T YOU TOLD ANYONE?

JUST THE FOLKS I'M CLOSE TO.

WHICH IS LESS'N YOU MIGHT THINK...

IT'S--

I KNOW, I KNOW.

IT'S THE SOUTH.

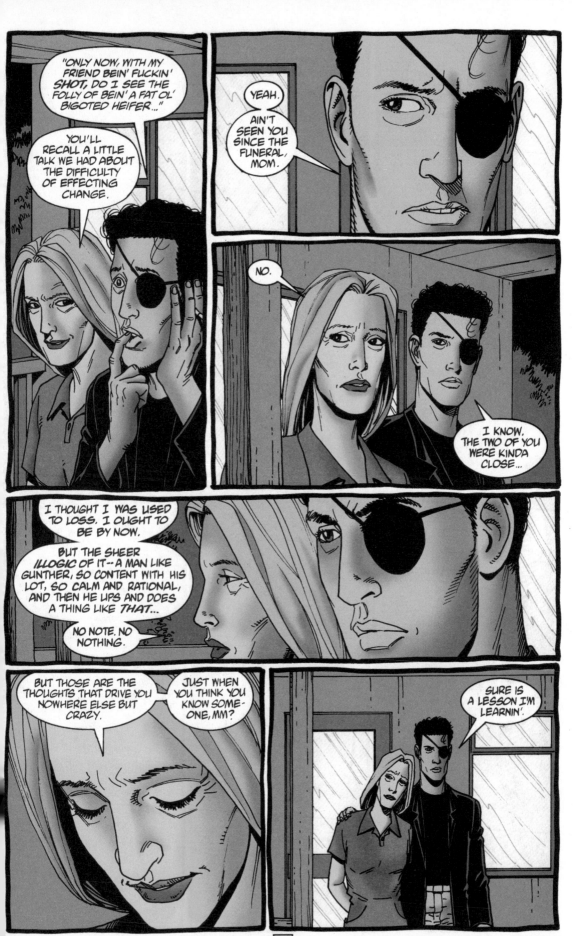

WHAT ARE YOU GOING TO DO?

WELL, I BEEN THINKIN' ABOUT THAT.

I'M GONNA GO FIND OUT SOME THINGS I NEED TO KNOW, AN' THEN I'M GONNA FINISH THIS JOB I GOTTA DO.

AN' THEN I'M GONNA BRING MY DARLIN' HOME TO MEET MY MOM.

WELL, IT'S A COLD, HARD WORLD OUT THERE, JESSE CUSTER. YOU TAKE CARE IN IT, D'YOU HEAR ME?

OH MOM, IT AIN'T THAT HARSH A WORLD, TRULY IT AIN'T...

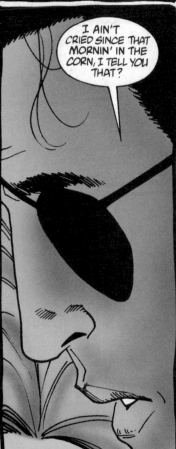

I AIN'T CRIED SINCE THAT MORNIN' IN THE CORN, I TELL YOU THAT?

BUT SOMETIMES I SURELY DO COME CLOSE.

THERE'S ONE LAST THING.

I KEPT THIS WITH ME ALWAYS. IT WAS WITH ME WHEN I WENT INTO THE SWAMP, AND ALL THROUGH THE ASYLUM, ALTHOUGH BY THEN I HAD NO IDEA WHY.

WHEN I CAME HERE I PUT IT IN A DRAWER AND FORGOT ABOUT IT. AND THEN YOU ARRIVED.

YOUR FATHER GAVE ME THIS FOR YOU THE NIGHT BEFORE HE DIED. JUST IN CASE, HE TOLD ME.

FOR WHEN YOU WERE A MAN.

MOM...

THIS HERE'S THE MEDAL OF HONOR.

SO I WAS GONNA STOP BY AN' SEE YOU TOMORROW, 'FORE I LEFT.

YEAH, YEAH.

I KNOW YOUR KIND. GONE LIKE A THIEF IN THE NIGHT IS MORE LIKE IT.

heh.

LOOK, uh...IF I CAUSED YOU TO THINK SOMETHIN' WAS GONNA HAPPEN HERE...I MEAN I KNOW WE GOT KINDA CLOSE...

OH JESSE, IF FLIRTIN'S A CRIME THEN YOU BETTER DEPUTIZE YOUR MOM AN' HAVE HER LOCK US BOTH UP...!

I KNEW YOUR PROBLEM RIGHT AFTER THAT NIGHT IN YOUR OFFICE. NEXT MORNIN', I BROUGHT IT UP, YOU CHANGED THE SUBJECT JUST AS QUICK AS YOU COULD.

MY PROBLEM...?

YOU'RE IN LOVE WITH SOMEBODY ELSE, JESSE.

YOU CAN TELL THAT?

uh-huh.

DAMN.

GOODNIGHT AND GOD BLESS

GARTH ENNIS - Writer   **STEVE DILLON - Artist**

PAMELA RAMBO - Colorist   **CLEM ROBINS - Letterer**   **AXEL ALONSO - Editor**

PREACHER created by GARTH ENNIS and STEVE DILLON

RAGE, BLOW, YOU CATARACTS AND HURRICANES!!

"KING LEAR."

ALWAYS WANTED TO SAY IT.

FIRST CONTACT

GARTH ENNIS - Writer   **STEVE DILLON** - Artist

PAMELA RAMBO - Colorist   CLEM ROBINS - Letterer   AXEL ALONSO - Editor

PREACHER created by GARTH ENNIS and STEVE DILLON

SKEETER, WHY DON'T YOU JUST RUN ALONG AN' HIDE IN THE TRUCK, HUH? I'M JUST 'BOUT TO SWALLOW A BIG DOSE OF HALLUCINOGENS AN' THINGS'RE APT TO GET A LITTLE STRANGE AROUND HERE...

MM?

NO?

YOUR FUNERAL, BUDDY.

THERE'S THINGS I GOTTA KNOW, SEE. EVERYTHING FROM FALLIN' OUTTA THAT DAMN PLANE TO WAKIN' UP IN THE DESERT, ALL THAT IS LOST TO ME.

AN' THEN THERE'S THE REASON I GOT THIS HERE PEYOTE IN THE FIRST PLACE, WHICH IS GENESIS. GODDAMN SPOOK'S BEEN IN MY HEAD THE BEST PART'VE A YEAR, AN' I STILL AIN'T NO NEARER USIN' IT TO TRACK DOWN THE LORD...

SO MAYBE THIS SHIT'LL HELP ME FIND THE WAY.

HERE WE GO, I GUESS.

JUST HOPE IT AIN'T LIKE IN THAT GODDAMN DOORS MOVIE.

BOY DID IT SUCK.

WUFF.

WUFF! WUFF! *WUFF!*

YEAH, BUT...AIN'T NO ONE GONNA BOTHER US, ALL THE WAY OUT HERE...

DAMN...

IS IT S'POSED TO MAKE YORE FINGERS SEE-THROUGH?

OR IS IT?

NOT?

I MEAN... *HEY...!*

GODDAMN, WHAT'S-- SHIT--

WHAT THE FUCK IS--

HOW'RE YEH!

CASS...?

SORT OF. MORE THE WAY YEH SEE ME, TO BE HONEST WITH YEH.

THIS IS YER BRAIN SHOWIN' YEH WHAT YEH EXPECT TO SEE, RIGHT? SO IT'S GOT ME SET UP AS A NASTY, SLIMY, GIRLFRIEND-STEALIN', BLOODSUCKIN', HORRIBLE WEE *LEECH*...

THAT AIN'T HOW I SEE YOU!

ISN'T IT?

WELL-- NO--I MEAN--

JESUS, THIS IS FUCKED-UP...

COURSE IT'S FUCKED-UP, YEH EEJIT! YEH'VE THE BASTARD OFFSPRING OF A DEMON AN' AN ANGEL LIVIN' IN YER MIND AS A SPIRITUAL ENTITY--YEH DIDN'T THINK THIS WAS GONNA BE A *NORMAL* PEYOTE TRIP, DID YEH?

WHAT-EVER THE FUCK THAT IS...

GODDAMMIT, CASS... KNOCK IT OFF...

ULK-- ULK-- ULK--

SORRY, JESSE-- *URRPP!* I CAN'T HELP IT, IT'S IN ME NATURE!

OH! WATCH YEH DON'T PASS OUT FROM LOSS OF BLOOD, THERE!

SHE WOULDN'T! NOT HER! NOT TULIP, NOT WITH A PIECE'VE FUCKIN' SHIT LIKE YOU!

BUT ISN'T THAT HOW YOU SEE ME NOW, JESSE? DOWN AMONGST THE SHIT? A FILTHY LITTLE SLUT WHO'D GIVE HERSELF TO *ANYONE*?

YOU *HATE* ME FOR WHAT I'VE DONE, THE VERY THOUGHT OF ME *DISGUSTS* YOU...

IT'S A *VISION*, DUMBASS. AIN'T YOU GOT THAT YET?

NO! *NEVER!* NOT IN A GODDAMNED LIFE-TIME! FUCK ALLA THAT SHIT, AN' IF THERE IS A PARTA ME WOULD EVER THINK THAT-- *FUCK IT TOO!*

YOU COCKSUCKER, JODY! I'LL KICK YOUR ASS A THOUSAND TIMES!!

EVERYONE HOLDS DARKNESS IN THEIR HEART, JESSE CUSTER. DON'T EVER FORGET THAT WE ARE THE DARKNESS IN YOURS.

JODY?

GIT ON ABOUT YORE DAMN VISION, BOY.

OH JESUS-- THIS IS IT--

THIS IS IT--

!

FOR THE GREAT HEREAFTER--

THIS LOOKS A HELL OF A LOT LIKE UTAH.

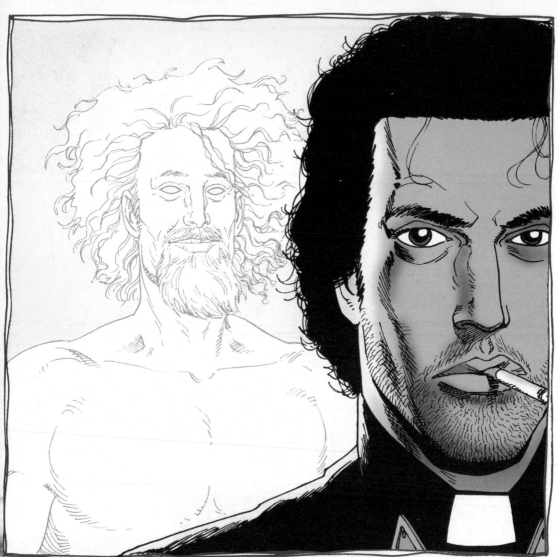

I GUESS YOU'D BE THE LORD.

REJOICE.

FOR YOU WHO WERE LOST ARE FOUND AGAIN. YOU WHO STOOD AT THE GATES OF DEATH ARE SAVED BY MY MOST MERCIFUL HAND.

YOU, MY SON.

I AIN'T YOUR GODDAMN SON.

YOU ARE HUMAN, JESSE. MEN AND WOMEN ARE MY SONS AND DAUGHTERS, AND EVER WAS IT SO.

REJOICE IN THIS. REJOICE THAT I HAVE SAVED YOU FROM YOUR FATAL FALL. AND YET REJOICE STILL FURTHER.

FOR I DO LOVE YOU STILL.

TWICE BEFORE I HAVE WARNED YOU. TWICE BEFORE I HAVE COME TO YOUR COMPANIONS, ENTRUSTED THEM WITH MESSAGES.

AND SEE, THEY HAVE CROSSED ONCE MORE. AND BECAUSE I AM A JUST GOD, AND A MERCIFUL GOD, AND MOST OF ALL A LOVING GOD--

"TELL HIM TO TURN BACK, TO END HIS SEARCH." "TELL HIM TO LEAVE ME BE, OR THE THIRD TIME OUR PATHS CROSS I SHALL DESTROY HIM."

YOU ARE FORGIVEN.

YOUR LONG JOURNEY IS AT LAST AT AN END. YOU HAVE FOUND YOUR LORD: I STAND BEFORE YOU, WONDROUS, LOVING, GRACIOUS, FULL OF LIGHT. YOU NEED SEEK NO LONGER.

GO NOW AND LIVE IN PEACE.

THE FUCK I WILL, MISTER.

YOU WILL NOT ACCEPT MY BLESSING...?

I AIN'T ACCEPTIN' SHIT FROM YOU.

THERE'S QUESTIONS YOU GOTTA ANSWER. NOT JUST WHY CREATION'S FULLA PAIN AN' MISERY, OR WHY YOU'D MAKE A WORLD THIS COLD.

NO, YOU TELL ME WHY YOU'RE RUNNIN' FROM ME, BOY. TELL ME WHAT GIVES YOU THE RIGHT TO DESERT YOUR PLACE IN HEAVEN, TO RUN OUT ON FOLKS YOU MEAN SO MUCH TO.

AN' TELL ME WHY I SHOULDN'T *SEND YOUR ASS RIGHT BACK THERE.*

THE CREATION CANNOT MAKE DEMANDS OF ITS CREATOR...!

THEN THE CREATOR SHOULDN'T PISS ON HIS CREATION.

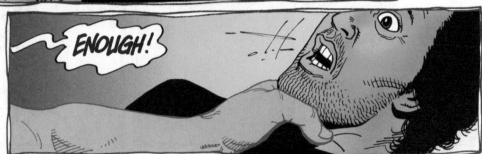

ANSWER
OR BE--

YOU

WANT IT
QUICK?

MAY AS WELL,
PREACHER.

YOU'RE
DYIN' ANY-
HOW.

DYIN'...?

AIN'T MANY SURVIVE THE TOUCH OF GOD, BOY. SAINTS, MOSTLY. MAYBE A PROPHET OR TWO.

YOU DID LIVE YOU'D GO CRAZY. AIN'T NO WAY YOU'D REMEMBER ANY OF THIS.

BUT YOU DON'T LOOK TO ME LIKE YOU'RE GONNA LIVE THROUGH IT...

OH-- YEAH--?

I AIN'T DYIN'. AIN'T GOIN' CRAZY. AN' I BY GOD *WILL* REMEMBER, ONE WAY OR THE OTHER.

I DON'T NEED NO QUICK WAY OUT FROM YOU.

'CAUSE YOU AN' ME--

GONNA TAKE THAT BASTARD--

DOWN...

I AIN'T HELPIN' YOU WITH NOTHIN', PREACHER.

SO LONG.

YOU JUST DID...BIG MAN...

YOU... JUST... DID...

211

O.

WHOA--!

WUFF!

OH, YOU GOOD DOG, YOU! YOU GOOD LITTLE GUY!

I SWEAR...

WUFF-WUFF-WUFF!

SAW IT IN HIS EYES, SKEET.

ALL THEM THINGS WERE LOST TO ME THAT I KNOW NOW, AN' THAT'S WHAT STANDS OUT MOST.

THE LOOK IN HIS GODDAMN EYES.

IT AIN'T HOW I USE GENESIS TO FIND HIM; IT'S THE OTHER WAY AROUND.

WHY'D HE GIVE ME ALL THEM CHANCES TO QUIT, ONLY TO COME OUT AN' CONFRONT ME HIM-SELF? WHY COULDN'T HE STAY AWAY?

HELL, MAY AS WELL ASK *WHY GOD WOULD CREATE THE DAMN WORLD IN THE FIRST PLACE...*

OH.

AN' I KNOW WHAT HE'S SCARED OF, TOO.

PREACHER
BINSON • SALVA
INHAMP • DAVI
MENECH • JAMES
RDIFFI • GARETH
RRIDGE • MIKE
BURNSON • ALAN
ZZARD • JUAN

THE LAND OF BAD THINGS

GARTH ENNIS - Writer   **STEVE DILLON - Artist**

PAMELA RAMBO - Colorist   CLEM ROBINS - Letterer   AXEL ALONSO - Editor

PREACHER created by GARTH ENNIS and STEVE DILLON

VINCENT R GORING

CE · JEFFRY HEF

HEY, SPACEMAN.

YOU TOO. STILL A PREACHER, HUH?

AIN'T THE KINDA JOB YOU WALK AWAY FROM, I GUESS. HOW 'BOUT YOU, HOW YOU DOIN'?

OKAY. MY LITTLE GIRL JOANIE, SHE EXPECTIN' AGAIN. MY YOUNGEST, WILLIAM JUNIOR, HE JUST QUIT HIGH SCHOOL. SAYS HE GONNA BE EAST COAST HANDBALL CHAMPION AN' HE GOTTA WORK ON HIS GAME.

DIDN'T EVEN KNOW THEY HAD A CHAMPION...

JUST ABOUT. WILLIAM AN' HIS FOOL FRIENDS BUSTIN' THEY ASSES ALL DAY ON THEM COURTS AT CONEY ISLAND, WAITIN' FOR A GODDAMN HANDBALL LEAGUE AIN'T NEVER GONNA AMOUNT TO SHIT.

SHIT, NO MUTHAFUCKA EVER MADE A CENT OFFA THAT STOOPID GAME...

NEVER CAN TELL WHEN IT COMES TO MONEY, SPACE.

NO. BUT YOU CAN MAKE A EDUCATED GUESS. THAT'S WHY FOLKS INVEST IN GOLD FUTURES, 'STEADA IN POWDERED BUFFALO SHIT.

STILL, I GUESS IT BEATS THE BOY SMOKIN' CRACK OR JOININ' SOME GODDAMN GANGSTA SET.

OR WORSE...

SHIT, LISTEN TO ME.

THAT'S WHY I'M HERE. I APPRE-CIATE YOU COMIN' TO MEET ME LIKE THIS : I KNOW IT'S A INCONVENIENCE...

NOT FOR JOHN CUSTER'S BOY IT AIN'T.

V.A. PASSED ON YOUR LETTER LAST WEEK, I HAD SOME VACATION TIME COMIN', AN'...WELL, I NEVER ACTUALLY BEEN HERE BEFORE.

NO?

DAMN, I GOT ONE JUST LIKE THAT.

NO, TO ME THAT WAR'S JUST A BUNCHA MEMORIES. I NEVER THOUGHTA IT AS SOMETHIN' AS OFFICIAL AS THIS, WIT' STATUES AN' FLAGS AN' THE WALL...

SEE WHO I FOUND?

FUCK

VINCENT A. GORING... IS THAT GONNY?

HOW 'BOUT THAT, HUH? CRAZY LITTLE FUCKER'S IMMORTAL.

LET'S YOU AN' ME TAKE US A WALK.

SO HOW YOU LOSE A DAMN EYE, ANYHOW?

PREACHIN'!

I BET. SOME CHURCH YOU GOT GOIN' THERE, REVEREND.

IT HAS ITS MOMENTS. FOUND MY *MOM*, THOUGH, WHICH WAS GOOD 'CAUSE I NEVER EXPECTED TO SEE HER AGAIN. SHE HAD SOMETHIN' FOR ME FROM MY DADDY.

I WAS HOPIN' YOU COULD TELL ME A LITTLE ABOUT IT.

WELL...THEY PROBABLY GOT THE CITATION IN CONGRESSIONAL RECORDS...

THEY PROBABLY DO, BUT IT'S THE HIGHEST AWARD THIS COUNTRY CAN GIVE YOU. I GUESS I'D LIKE TO KNOW HOW HE GOT IT.

FROM SOMEONE WAS ACTUALLY THERE.

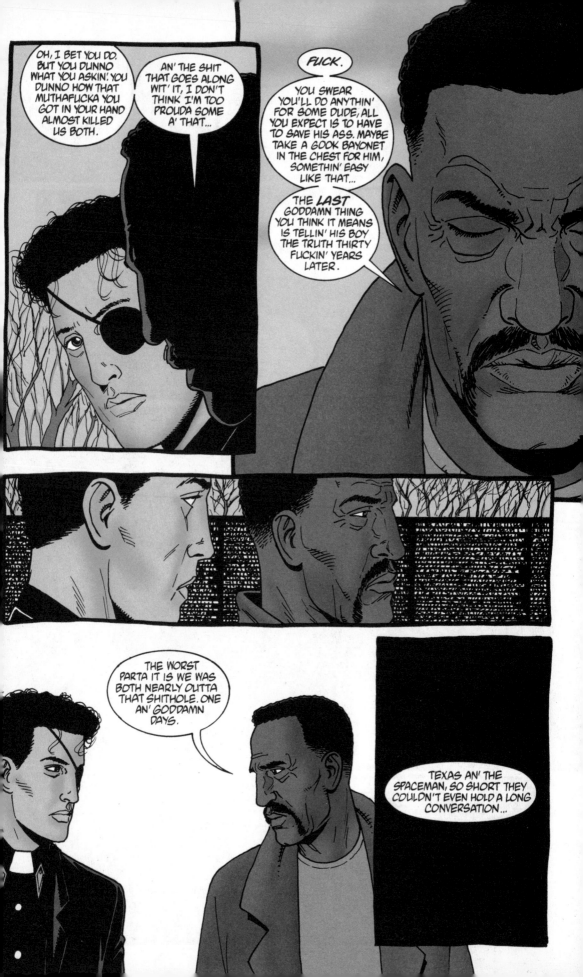

RUN FOR YOUR FUCKIN' LIVES!!

WHOLE FUCKIN' N.V.A. BATTALION--

FALL BACK! C'MON, GET THE FUCK OUT--

CAP'N, SARGE, FUCK, HEEELLP--

AAAAAHHH

THEY LEAVIN'! THEY DUSTIN' OFF, I FUCKIN' HEAR 'EM!

ONLY TWO! THIRD SLICK'S STILL WAITIN' FOR US!

JESUS CHRIST--!

WE'RE GONNA MAKE IT!

THEY STOPPED SHOOTIN'...

MUSTA DONE ALL THE WOUNDED.

FUCKIN' SLOPE COCKSUCKERS--!

WHOA, OL' HOSS. YOU WANNA TAKE ALLA THEM ON, YOU MAY AS WELL RUN OUT THERE WAVIN' YOUR PECKER.

HOW'S THAT?

KINDA NUMB JESUS!!

YOU FELT THAT, I GUESS I AIN'T GONNA HAVE TO AMPUTATE JUST YET...

MUTHA-FUCK--!

I THOUGHT IT WAS CLEAN, IT WENT RIGHT FUCKIN' THROUGH...

IT WAS 'TIL WE RAN THROUGH THAT SWAMP FULLA DEAD HOGS AN' MONKEY SHIT AN' ALL KINDSA AWFUL BUGS. YOU PROBABLY GOT A GODDAMN PLAGUE FACTORY SET UP IN THERE RIGHT NOW.

GOOD NEWS IS, I AIN'T EVEN GOT A SCRATCH.

YOU ONE ETERNAL RAY OF HOPE, TEXAS. ANY MUTHAFUCKA EVER TELL YOU THAT?

WELL, LET'S THINK 'BOUT WHAT WE *DO* GOT GOIN' FOR US: WE GOT NEARLY ALLA OUR SHIT, AN' YOU GRABBED YOUR PACK WHEN THEY HIT US SO WE GOT C-RATS FOR MAYBE THREE OR FOUR DAYS...

AN' WE GOT THIS HERE MAP I TOOK OFFA CAP'N LINDSAY, WHICH IS GONNA COME IN REAL USEFUL ON THE WALK HOME.

WHAT?

HE'S DEAD, SPACE. HE AIN'T GONNA NEED IT.

NO, I MEAN *WALK HOME?* YOU GONE FUCKIN' CRAZY? GOTTA BE TWO HUNDRED KLICKS FROM HERE TO KHE SAN, AT LEAST!

YEAH, BUT IT AIN'T EVEN HALFA THAT TO VAHN LO, HERE, WHERE IT LOOKS LIKE THE ARMY GOT SOME KINDA FORWARD OUTPOST. LAST PARTA IT ISN'T EVEN JUNGLE.

SHIT, MAN, IT'S STILL A FUCKIN' LONG WAY...! AN' I GOT THIS FUCKED-UP LEG, TOO!

WELL THE ALTERNATIVE IS TO SURRENDER, AN' THAT MEANS LETTIN' THESE SONSA-BITCHES TAKE US BACK UP NORTH TO GIVE UNCLE HO BLOW JOBS FOR THE RESTA OUR LIVES.

THAT AIN'T FOR US.

WE'RE DOWN TO FORTY DAYS AN' A WAKE-UP.

WE'RE GOIN' HOME.

229

WE AIN'T HERE TO WIN NO FUCKIN' WAR, WE AIN'T HERE TO *BEAT* NO ONE...

WHAT DO WE DO, WE BUILD A BUNCHA GODDAMN FIREBASES OUT IN THE BUSH AN' THE HUEYS FLY US IN AN' OUT, AN' ONCE WE GET A COUPLE K.I.A. CONFIRMED WE GO BACK AN' LIE ON OUR ASSES 'TIL IT'S TIME TO DO IT AGAIN.

THAT AIN'T HOW YOU WIN; YOU'RE S'POSED TO TAKE AN' HOLD TERRITORY AN' THEN TAKE SOME MORE...

AN' POLICE ACTION *MY ASS,* NOBODY'S TELLIN' ME WE'RE PRO-TECTIN' SHIT OUT HERE. HALF THE VILLES WE WALK INTO WE BURN TO THE FUCKIN' GROUND.

I BEEN TRYNNA THINK OF IT LIKE A BAD DREAM, I GUESS.

HOW SO?

WELL, WAY IT'S S'POSED TO WORK IS, YOU WORK REAL HARD AN' YOU'RE REWARDED WITH A GOOD LIFE AN' THE FREEDOM TO ENJOY IT. THAT'S AMERICA, OKAY? THAT'S HOW I ALWAYS UNDERSTOOD IT.

AN' MY DADDY, WHO WAS A MARINE BACK IN WORLD WAR TWO AN' FOUGHT ON GUADALCANAL AN' OKINAWA AN' ALL KINDSA TERRIBLE PLACES, HE TOLD ME SOMETIMES YOUR COUNTRY DEMANDS A PRICE FOR THEM THINGS. SOMETIMES YOU GOTTA GO OFF AN' FIGHT.

BUT THAT WAS OKAY WITH ME, 'CAUSE TO ME MY COUNTRY WAS WORTH IT.

BUT *THIS*...BEIN' FED INTO THIS GODDAMN MEAT-GRINDER, ANY FOOL CAN SEE THIS DON'T DO AMERICA NO GOOD AT ALL. AN' I DON'T KNOW WHO THE HELL WOULD WANT US HERE, WHO'D BE HAPPY AT SO MANY BOYS BEIN' SENT OUT HERE TO DIE, BUT I DO KNOW IT'S NOBODY GOOD...

SO I TRY TO BELIEVE IT'S LIKE THIS OVER HERE IN 'NAM--BUT THEN YOU GO HOME AN' WAKE UP AN' IT'S BACK TO THE WAY THINGS *WERE*. THE GOOD WAY, IN THE COUNTRY PLAYS FAIR BY YOU IF YOU PLAY FAIR BY IT.

THE NIGHTMARE'S OVER, I SAY TO MYSELF.

EXCEPT IT'S JUST BEGINNIN', AN' THERE AIN'T NO WAKIN' UP FROM IT.

'CAUSE IT WAS OUR COUNTRY THAT SENT US HERE.

SO I LOOKED AT THIS KID FROM WEST TEXAS, FEELIN' ALL CUT UP AN' BETRAYED 'CAUSE HE SUDDENLY REALIZED THE LAND OF THE FREE BEEN FUCKIN' HIM IN THE ASS ALL HIS LIFE--

AN' I TOLD MYSELF, SHIT, SO THAT'S WHAT IT'S LIKE TO BE THE WHITE BOY.

ANY NIGGA YOU ASK CAN TELL YOU THAT'S HOW AMERICA WORKS.

SO WHAT YOU GONNA DO NOW YOU THINK EVERYTHING'S SO SHITTY?

HELL, I'M GONNA ROTATE HOME FROM THE LAND OF BAD THINGS AN' FIND ME A SWEET LITTLE GAL WITH BIG BROWN EYES, AN' WE GONNA FUCK LIKE JACKRABBITS FOR THE RESTA OUR NATURAL LIVES.

WE GONNA RAISE A WHOLE LOTTA KIDS, STARTIN' WITH A BOY, I RECKON...

AN' ANY TIME I HAVE TO, I'LL FIGHT LIKE HELL FOR THEM.

SO I LOOKED AT THIS KID FROM WEST TEXAS AGAIN, DRAGGIN' MY CRIPPLED ASS THROUGH THE BOONIES, NEVER EVEN HEARDA QUITTIN'--

AN' I TOLD MYSELF TO SHUT THE FUCK UP.

I AIN'T GONNA MAKE IT...

BULLSHIT.

LEG'S FUCKED. CAN'T WALK NO MORE. YOU GOTTA LEAVE ME.

BULLSHIT.

TEXAS, YOU... YOU GONNA GET YOURSELF KILLED OUT HERE FOR NUTHIN'. I'M DEAD ANYWAYS.

BULLSHIT.

FUCK YOU.

WHAT THE FUCK'RE YOU *DOIN'*?

...

WHAT THE FUCK'RE *YOU* DOIN'?

DROP THE FUCKIN' GUN! QUIT IT!

YOU OUTTA YOUR FUCKIN' MIND? YOU GONNA KILL ME TO STOP ME FROM SHOOTIN' MYSELF?

PUT IT THE FUCK DOWN!

FUCK YOU! YOU CRAZY, MAN! I'M TRYNNA SAVE YOUR DUMB ASS FROM DYIN' IN THIS MUTHA-FUCKIN' JUNGLE AN' NOW YOU PULLIN' THIS SHIT! WHAT THE *FUCK*!

FUCK *YOU*, BOY! I AIN'T HAULED YOU HALFWAY ACROSS HELL'S CREATION JUST SO YOU CAN PUSSY OUT ON ME NOW! YOU CAN'T JUST THROW IT ALL AWAY LIKE THIS, *THIS IS FUCKED*!

NO, *YOU*! YOU FUCKED! *YOU* STOOPID FUCKIN' REDNECK, I NEVER ASKED YOU FOR SHIT AN' I AIN'T FUCKIN' ASKIN' *NOW*!!

WHY YOU BLACK SON OF A BITCH, I DON'T BELIEVE YOU FUCKIN' SAID THAT! YOU PULL THIS SHIT ON *ME*, NOW, AFTER EVERYTHING WE FUCKIN' BEEN THROUGH!

MUTHAFUCKA, I'M FUCKIN' TELLIN' YOU TO FUCKIN' LEAVE ME!

YOU IGNORANT PIGFUCKIN' WHITE TRASH COCKSUCKER, I DON'T NEED YOUR MUTHA- FUCKIN' CRACKER ASS HELPIN' ME! YOU GO AN' FUCK YOURSELF, WHITE BOY! FUCK YOU AN' ALL YOUR FUCKIN' KIND!

THE HELL WITH YOU, NIGGER! YOU FUCKIN' JUNGLE BUNNY! I WOULDN'T HELP YOU IF YOU WERE THE RICHEST COON IN HARLEM AN' YOUR EVERY FUCKIN' TOOTH WAS SOLID GOLD!

YOU WANNA, GO ON AN' PULL THAT TRIGGER.

'CAUSE THINGS'RE REALLY AS SHITTY AS THIS, I'M GONNA BE RIGHT BEHIND YOU.

I SEE BUNKERS, JEEP OR TWO...LOOKS LIKE THEY EVEN GOT A COUPLE TANKS DUG IN OVER THERE...

I DON'T SEE NO CHOPPER.

WAY I SEE IT, ONLY WAY WE GOT TO SIGNAL 'EM IS FIRIN' SHOTS IN THE AIR. AN' ALL THIS GODDAMN BUSH IS GONNA BE CRAWLIN' WITH GOOK O.P.'S AN' SNIPERS.

NO, I THINK WE'RE GONNA HAVE TO GO TO THEM...

ACROSS THAT OPEN GROUND?

AFTER DARK.

WELL. THAT IS A PROBLEM.

YEAH, BUT...TEXAS, MAN, THIS FUCKIN' LEG GONNA DROP OFF ANYTIME! CHARLIE DON'T SMELL US COMIN', HE SURE AS FUCK GONNA SEE US WHEN THE SUN COMES UP AN' WE ONLY GONE TWENNY FUCKIN' YARDS!

I COULD GET USED TO THIS...

SHUT THE FUCK UP!

YES SIR, ONLY MUTHA-FUCKIN' WAY TO TRAVEL...

JESUS!

ANYTHING OUT THERE, SERGEANT?

NO SIR.

WELL, STAY ON IT. YOU KNOW CHARLIE.

YES SIR, CAPTAIN HOLDEN.

AN' THIS NEXT PART I'LL NEVER BELIEVE 'TIL MY DYIN' FUCKIN' DAY, BUT IT'S HOW YOU WIN' THE MEDAL OF HONOR.

NOT AT US! HOLD YOUR FIRE!

JESUS CHRIST, WE'RE FUCKIN' AMERICANS!!

THEY'RE WHO?

I SAID I THINK THEY'RE MARINES, SIR!

WELL THAT FIGURES--

WHO ELSE'D BE DUMB ENOUGH TO TRY WALKING IN THROUGH A GODDAMNED MINEFIELD?

OKAY, GET 'EM OUT OF HERE! GO!

THAT TANK CAP'N, HE WAS THE ONE WROTE UP JOHN'S CITATION, AFTER HE TALKED TO ME LATER ON.

FUCKIN' UP A COMPANY-STRENGTH *V.C.* ATTACK, HELPIN' A WOUNDED COMRADE ACROSS A HUNDRED KLICKS OF ENEMY TERRITORY, *AND* BRINGIN' HIM IN UNDER FIRE--THAT WAS MORE'N ENOUGH.

THEY WAS TAKIN' US INTO VAHN LO TO WAIT FOR A MEDEVAC, BOTH OF US SHOT FULLA MORPHINE, AN' ALL OF A SUDDEN I COULD HEAR SOMEONE SAYIN' MY NAME...

THIS AIN'T OUR TIME TO DIE.

THEN I PASSED OUT AN' NEVER SAW HIM AGAIN.

I WAS SHOT UP WORSE'N HE WAS, AN' IT TOOK A COUPLE OPERATIONS BY A SPECIALIST 'FORE THEY WAS SURE I COULD KEEP THE LEG.

BY THEN TEXAS WAS OUTTA THE HOSPITAL AN' POSTED DOWN TO DA NANG, FINISHIN' HIS TOUR ON SOME KINDA BULLSHIT MILK RUN. AN' BY THE TIME I WAS DOIN' THE SAME THING HE GOT SENT HOME.

BUT YOU KNOW SOMETHIN'? HE *SAW IT.* IN THEM SIX LITTLE WORDS HE SAW THROUGH TO THE CLEAR, PURE-D TRUTH THAT SHOULDA MATTERED MORE TO ME THAN ANYTHING.

ALL THIS TIME I BEEN FUCKED UP AN' MAD ABOUT THE SHIT WENT DOWN OVER THERE, WONDERIN' WHY ALL THEM DUDES GOT WASTED AN' I MADE IT, CURSIN' THE GOVERNMENT FOR FUCKIN' US LIKE THAT... AN' IT'S ONLY NOW I CAN SEE LIKE HE DID.

WE MADE IT.

WE DIDN'T END UP ON NO WALL.

I WANNA THANK YOU, SPACE.

YEAH?

YEAH. SEE, I GOT A JOB TO DO...

AN' FOR THE FIRST TIME EVER I KNOW WHAT I GOTTA DO TO FINISH IT.

BUT I SWEAR, KNOWIN' MY DADDY WON THAT THING, I COULDN'TA TAKEN ANOTHER STEP UNTIL I FOUND OUT HOW.

IT HELPS TO KNOW THE KINDA MAN YOU GOTTA MEASURE UP TO.

IT GIVES YOU HOPE.

YOU GONNA STAY A WHILE?

YEAH, I ...

I KINDA LIKE IT HERE.

I LIKE HOW THEY GOT THE GRUNTS' NAMES UP, ALL OF 'EM, STEADA JUST THE DATESA THE WAR OR SOME SHIT. AN' I LIKE HOW IT'S QUIET HERE.

AN' I 'SPECIALLY LIKE HOW THEY GOT THEM THREE DUDES IN THE TREES OVER THERE, LIKE THEY COMIN' OUTTA THE BOONIES AFTER SOME PATROL, AN' THEY ONLY JUST SEEN ALLA THIS--

AN' THEY LIKE, "MUTHA*FUCKA*..."

"SOMEONE REMEMBERED."

VINCENT R GORIN

SO TELL ME
SOMETHIN'.

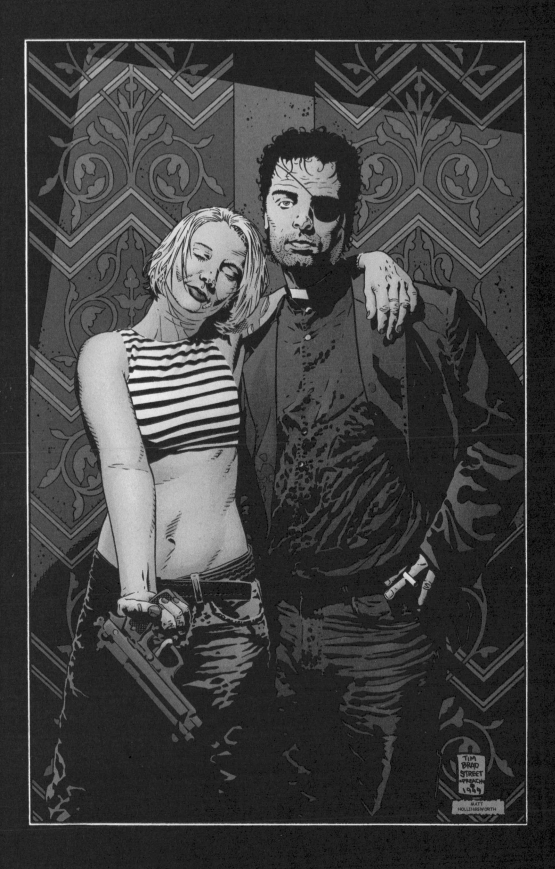